Kathleen *and*
Christopher

Oct. 1911

dear Mother
Just a little ~~froll~~ Note to
you. I have packed up the
dolls ~~house~~ house it is broken.
Love ~~from~~ from your
Loveing Son
Christopher

x x x x x x x x x
+ + x x + + +
+ x x + + + + +
+ + x x x x x +
+ x x x x x x
x x x x + +

KISS TREE
FOR
KBE

# Kathleen *and* Christopher

## CHRISTOPHER ISHERWOOD'S LETTERS TO HIS MOTHER

Christopher Isherwood

EDITED BY
LISA COLLETTA

 University of Minnesota Press | Minneapolis | London

Frontispiece: Letter to Kathleen written by Christopher in 1911, when he was seven years old.

All letters are reproduced and quoted with permission from Don Bachardy. Copyright by the Estate of Christopher Isherwood.

Letters from Christopher Isherwood to Kathleen Isherwood are reproduced by permission of the Huntington Library, San Marino, California. [Isherwood, Christopher, to Kathleen Bradshaw Isherwood, CI 1192-1298, CI 1257, 1260, 1265, notes from W. H. (Wystan Hugh) Auden]

Correspondence of W. H. Auden is reprinted with permission. Copyright by the Estate of W. H. Auden.

All photographs and images are reproduced with permission from Don Bachardy and by permission of the Huntington Library, San Marino, California. Copyright by the Estate of Christopher Isherwood.

Published by the University of Minnesota Press
111 Third Avenue South, Suite 290
Minneapolis, MN 55401-2520
http://www.upress.umn.edu

Library of Congress Cataloging-in-Publication Data

Isherwood, Christopher, 1904–1986
    Kathleen and Christopher : Christopher Isherwood's letters to his mother / Christopher Isherwood ; edited by Lisa Colletta.
        p.    cm.
    Includes bibliographical references and index.
    ISBN 0-8166-4580-9 (alk. paper)
    1. Isherwood, Christopher, 1904–1986—Correspondence.    2. Bradshaw-Isherwood, Kathleen, 1868–1960—Correspondence.    3. Authors, English—20th century—Correspondence.    4. Mothers and sons—England.    I. Bradshaw-Isherwood, Kathleen, 1868–1960.    II. Colletta, Lisa.    III. Title.
    PR6017.S5Z486 2005
    823'.912—dc22

                                                                        2005011746

Printed in the United States of America on acid-free paper

The University of Minnesota is an equal-opportunity educator and employer.

12   11   10   09   08   07   06   05              10   9   8   7   6   5   4   3   2   1

# Contents

*vii*    Introduction
        *Lisa Colletta*

*xix*    Acknowledgments

  *3*    **1935**
        Copenhagen—Brussels—Amsterdam—Sintra, Portugal

 *43*    **1936**
        Sintra, Portugal—Ostende—Brussels

 *87*    **1937**
        Brussels—Luxembourg—Dover

 *97*    **1938**
        Paris—Marseilles—Djibouti—Ceylon—Singapore—
        Hong Kong—Canton—Hankow—Shanghai—"Empress
        of Asia"—Dover—Brussels

*121*    **1939**
        New Haven, Connecticut—New York City—
        Grand Canyon—Hollywood—Santa Monica

*163*    Editor's Notes

*179*    Index

# *Introduction*
## LISA COLLETTA

In Christopher Isherwood's idiosyncratic memoir of his parents, *Kathleen and Frank: The Autobiography of a Family,* he writes that it took him a long time to come to terms with his mother's influence on his life. For Isherwood, Kathleen embodied the past, and he had learned "to hate and fear the Past because it threatened to swallow his future" (10). He rebelled early against both the memory of his dead "hero-father" and the nostalgia and conventionality of his "demon" mother. Throughout his childhood, Isherwood's father represented unattainable perfection, becoming a mythical figure used by a tradition-bound mother to reproach him and keep him in line. For Kathleen, however, the past was almost by definition "happier," and the present would always be inferior to it. As a result, she was a chronicler of the past, and throughout her life she was a devoted and assiduous diarist, finding solace in her old age by taking out her diaries and reading them to herself in an attempt to relive happier days. For Isherwood, a love of the past was anathema; he deeply resented the expectations of his mother and his class and spent much of his life in anxious wandering, trying to escape them both. Ironically, he was unable to escape the influence of

Kathleen, and he too became a recorder, a writer who throughout his life—in one way or another—made himself the subject of most of his work. "And so," he became, like Kathleen, "willy-nilly, a celebrant of the Past" (10).

Given his preoccupation with his own past, Isherwood (who in his works often wrote of himself as a character or referred to himself in the third person) admits in *Kathleen and Frank* that "he finds it hard to explain to himself why he never asked Kathleen to let him read her diary while she was alive" (10). To readers of Isherwood, this isn't so surprising. He is quite damning of his mother and indeed of the entire legacy of the Bradshaw Isherwoods, of which she was so proud, and in his role as "anti-son" he was "afraid of getting entangled in the spider's web of her memory" (10). Of course, Isherwood was always caught in the web of Kathleen's memory, as a product of her and her class values, in reaction to her in his sexuality and his choice of a career, and in his use of her diaries and correspondence in his own writing. After writing *Mr Norris Changes Trains* and *Goodbye to Berlin,* Isherwood famously burned the diaries he kept while living in Germany. He writes in *Christopher and His Kind* that he did this because he feared the explicit account of his sex life might fall into the hands of the police or other enemies, but in looking back he found that excuse rather unconvincing. What he really suspected was that "he destroyed his real past because he preferred the simplified, more creditable, more exciting fictitious past which he had created to take its place" (40). It might also be said that he preferred to believe in a simplified, more creditable, and more exciting version of his relationship with Kathleen, one in which she never understood him, was always the Other, and always in opposition to him. However, the letters collected in this volume reveal a different, more affectionate re-lationship that complicates his idea of himself as the "anti-son." Here we have Isherwood's actual words to his mother, not those remembered or chosen by others—or indeed by himself—years later. Here Isherwood's complex and immensely important relationship with Kathleen is revealed as he lectures her, pleads with her, jokes with her, and worries about her. She is for him in turns an agent, a sounding board, and an unbreakable connection to England and his past.

In the 1970s, when he wrote about "Christopher's real past," Isherwood stated that he sorely missed the existence of his diaries, knowing that the Berlin novels falsify events and alter dates, and he comments that the few surviving letters "written at that time by Christopher and his friends to each other . . . usually have no dates at all" (40). Clearly, *Christopher and His Kind* is no more Isherwood's "real" past than is any other of his autobiographical works, and his comment about the few existing letters to his friends is revealing. Not only does he not mention Kathleen in the acknowledgments in that book—though he thanks almost everyone else from his Berlin years—but he seems to suggest through his comments that he had very little archival material to work with and ignores completely the existence and his use of these very detailed letters, all of which are dated and addressed. As readers will see here, Isherwood wrote to his mother nearly once a week, often more, and, though he is guarded, he relied on her greatly and kept her informed of most of his concerns. As Peter Parker has speculated in his recent biography, "Perhaps he preferred not to remember. It did not suit the scheme of that book to show Kathleen as someone who spent much of her time cooperating with her son rather than antagonizing him" (329).

This is hardly an indictment of Isherwood, however. As he himself wrote, "Art has transfigured life, and other people's art has transfigured Christopher's art" (59). Kathleen's art was her diary, and he admits that her diary is probably the most reliable source of information about those years in the thirties when he was trying so hard to exclude her. Isherwood's art was also writing, and his own life was his primary subject, as well, but his art demanded that he reinvent, dramatize, exaggerate, and play down the "real" when it didn't fit the purposes of his work. Parker notes that "Isherwood's relationship with the past was complicated," and if the past and his mother were virtually the same thing for him, his relationship with his mother is just as, if not more, complicated (3). In his writing it was important to portray Kathleen as the representative of the conventional world that thwarted his desires and wanted to turn him into an English don; every protagonist needs something to define himself against, and every plot needs a complication. But, if Isherwood was hard on Kathleen in the autobiographical works, he is hard on "Christopher," too. Indeed, all of his "characters" serve a larger aesthetic purpose, and he is arguably one of the bravest writers of the century in his willingness to reveal and dramatize his own personality and motivations, even when he himself found them unpleasant or disturbing. The value of these letters lay in the fact that he did not write them to dramatize himself or a plot— though a wonderful narrative arc emerges from them—but as immediate and direct communication. Readers and scholars of Isherwood will recognize many of the iconic moments related in the letters from his other works. He often quotes them in *Christopher and His Kind,* but, as Parker notes, he did so with a purpose in mind and left out or embellished events according to his plan. As Katherine Bucknell asserts, even Isherwood's most autobiographical writing is highly stylized, tipping over "from history into mythology," and indeed the diaries seem more self-consciously performed than do these letters (xi). Here we not only see another side of Isherwood, we also can read, in a continuous volume, the only extant personal writing from the time period; his diaries don't begin until 1939, overlapping a year with the letters but expressing a quite different narrative voice. These letters, therefore, are one of the few records we have of Isherwood's life at this time that isn't filtered through the lens of time and memory.

What an amazing time it was, too, not only in Isherwood's life but in the history of the past century. The letters cover a period when his life as a writer is taking shape and he is emerging—along with W. H. Auden and Stephen Spender—as one of the three young men who, according to Evelyn Waugh, "ganged up and captured the decade" (Parker 223). The letters are exciting and thought-provoking because they are an eyewitness account of Europe in the thirties by a keen observer. Writing, of course, without knowing the course events would take, Isherwood is frank about the political situation in Europe and the activism of his friends, and there is an immediacy in these letters that brings to life the confusion, hopes, and fears of the era. Writing his mother frequently, from Copenhagen, Brussels, Amsterdam, Paris, Portugal, China, New York, and Hollywood, he details his anxiety about his German lover, Heinz, his doubts about his writing and himself, and his feelings about critical responses to his work. He comments on other writers and friends of the family, tells Kathleen amusing—albeit censored—anecdotes about acquaintances, and outlines his expenses and the growing income from his writing in rather specific detail. This is Christopher as loving son, tempering his performance of himself with consideration for his mother's feelings and prejudices, yet still vulnerable to the temptations of storytelling. Just as Adam Phillips noted about Isherwood's diaries, in his eagerness to tell things for effect, the letters become little dramas in themselves, and these little dramas are set against the larger drama of the world heading toward war.

Of course, in these letters Isherwood is not as frank about himself or others as in the diaries and some of the other writings from the time. Nonetheless, they do offer another, important view of Isherwood. As a novelist with the temperament of a diary keeper and "the inclinations of an autobiographer," Isherwood, notes Phillips, created characters, often based on himself, who love what he calls playacting, "who charm and flirt and reinvent themselves whenever necessary and as much as possible." In the letters to Kathleen, Isherwood the actor and Isherwood the recorder of immediate experience are both evident. Using language that is at once concealing and revealing—indeed, revealing because it is concealing—this is an Isherwood we have not seen before. This is the Isherwood who begins nearly every letter with "My darling Mummy," the son who wants to charm and please his mother and allay her fears more often than he wants to defy her. Although readers of Isherwood are aware that his relationship with Kathleen was vexed and conflicted, he wasn't always quarreling with her. He wrote in his diary that "this feeling of being quite different in different places and with different people is very strong in me," and the feeling of role playing is probably most profound when one is dealing with a parent (Parker 392). Parker writes that "although Isherwood's principal role was that of a writer, whose relationship was with an audience he never met, he nevertheless liked a live audience, one to whom he could talk about his life and work, tell funny stories, and effortlessly entertain" (390). John Lehmann recalls Isherwood's visits to Totland and his "endlessly lecturing my Mother—to her fascination and delight—in a gentle, bright persuasive way that is his own patent for young and old disciples, explaining China, discussing America, describing W.H.A. and the lives of his friends" (Parker 390). He does all this with Kathleen as well, and in the letters she fulfills his need for a live audience; he clearly desires to inform, lecture, and entertain her, especially in the letters from Hollywood, when his philosophies and sense of himself are undergoing drastic revisions and he needs to try out his new ideas on someone.

Throughout the upheaval of the mid to late thirties, Isherwood went through remarkable changes, both as a writer and as a person, and these letters chronicle these changes and practically pinpoint that precise moment in time when he went from politically disengaged to spiritually engaged, from cynical European to earnest Californian. Despite the fact that the letters cover only five years, the shifts in tone, voice, and outlook from early 1935 to Christmas 1939 are enormous, and the letters offer readers of Isherwood and scholars a new perspective on this important era. Because there is already a rather large body of documentary work on Isherwood, including Katherine Bucknell's thoroughly edited *Diaries* and Peter Parker's exhaustive biography— not to mention Isherwood's own autobiographical works—I have chosen not to include yet another list of brief biographies of those mentioned in the letters. To most readers acquainted with Isherwood's life, the people and events mentioned will be easily recognizable, and it seemed to me redundant to repeat information that has already been published in various places with great thoroughness. I have footnoted the first mention of a person's name and referenced that first note whenever that person is mentioned again or when the reference isn't clear, and I have given brief background information when Isherwood refers to an event without explaining it. For the most part, however, I have let the letters speak for themselves and offered very little in the way of an interpretive apparatus. I have retained Isherwood's somewhat inconsistent spelling, capitalization, and punctuation, but, to prevent confusion, I have italicized the titles of works because he often refers to real people by their fictional character's name, which is also frequently the title of a book or story.

The letters begin in 1935, when Isherwood is trying desperately to obtain a new nationality for Heinz, as fascism's grip tightens around them and Hitler introduces conscription. Many of the letters have brief notes written by Heinz to Kathleen at the bottom of the page, and although Isherwood withholds specifics about his sexual relationship with Heinz (Parker notes that Kathleen was well aware of it), Isherwood is candid about the obstacles facing them. The letters provide another, more direct view of the experiences he later submits to artistic form in the autobiographical and fictional works and proffer the specific details involved in moving from Copenhagen to Amsterdam to Brussels to Portugal. He comments frequently on visits from friends, including E. M. Forster, his playwriting work with Auden, the books he is writing and reviewing, and the critical reception of *Mr Norris Changes Trains.* The year ends with Christmas greetings from Portugal scribbled at the bottom of the page from Tony Hyndman, Stephen Spender, and Heinz.

Correspondence from 1936 is full of details about life in Portugal, including descriptions of the English colony there and accounts of visits from Gerald Hamilton, Brian Howard and his boyfriend, Toni Altmann, the Sterns, the Burfords, and Kathleen herself, among others. Isherwood excoriates a rather complimentary and patriotic article by Graham Greene about the death of King George V, and there is a lot of publishing and financial detail, especially about the plays with Auden, all against the backdrop of Heinz's increasingly alarming political problems and the outbreak of the Spanish civil war. Forced to leave Portugal for various reasons, Isherwood and Heinz are back in Brussels at the end of the year, where Heinz has an operation on his nose.

The momentous year of 1937 contains the fewest letters. There is an account of meeting Auden in Paris on his way to Spain, and Isherwood's translation of Bertolt Brecht's *Threepenny Opera*. Heinz is arrested and sentenced to prison, forced labor, and military service, but Parker writes that Heinz's arrest left Isherwood bereft of purpose and with few options but to return to London, so clearly he wouldn't have needed to write to Kathleen. He finishes the year in Dover with Auden, working on *On the Frontier*.

The letters from 1938 contain those sent during the trip to China with Auden. These letters run the gamut from mundane plea for money to satirical observation, and several have brief but wry notes from Auden at the bottom of the page. Isherwood seems to try out ideas on Kathleen, as some of the observations he makes to her find their way into *Journey to a War*. In March, German troops enter Austria, causing Isherwood and Auden much worry. Returning from China, they go to New York, but Isherwood returns to London and then goes to Brussels. In September, Neville Chamberlain, Édouard Daladier, Benito Mussolini, and Adolf Hitler meet in Munich and partition Czechoslovakia, and Chamberlain returns to England declaring "Peace in our time." The year ends with a rather depressed-sounding letter from Brussels, where Auden and Isherwood are finishing the manuscript of *Journey to a War*.

The letters from 1939 are different in tone, following the pair's arrival in New York, where Auden finds success but Isherwood writes to his mother of loneliness, self-doubt, obtuse critics, the need for money, his increasing pacifism, and the fear of inevitable war. As he sets off across the continent by bus, he faithfully writes to Kathleen and with camera-like precision describes to her the vastness of the United States. The letters clearly reveal Isherwood trying to negotiate his ties to Europe and his mother, his fear for her and his brother Richard's safety, his disgust with Europe entering another conflagration, and his delight in Los Angeles and the freedom he finds there. His Los Angeles letters relate Hollywood gossip, the excitement of working at MGM, encounters with film stars, and trenchant observations of the culture and landscape. Near the end of the last letter from December 1939, Isherwood tells Kathleen:

> Slowly, I am getting around to the idea of writing again. But it won't be anything like what I have done so far. Philosophical, probably, and deeply religious! Very obscure. Full of visions and dreams. It sounds awful, doesn't it? Perhaps it's only a reaction from movie work.

This signals the conclusion of one phase and the beginning of another. This American half of Isherwood's life, the philosophical, religious,

Southern Californian life, would be chronicled in the diaries, a more introspective and overtly revealing literary form.

Isherwood's move to Hollywood changed his life and his writing. Turning his back on Europe and family ties, Isherwood committed himself to a new life. He quickly became a U.S. citizen, and, when he inherited the Marple estate upon the death of his uncle Henry in the summer of 1940, he gave the house and the money to his younger brother, Richard. Isherwood's energies turned inward in Southern California, and Bucknell asserts, "He wanted to remain in America so he could finish growing up," to grapple with himself and find out who he really was (xiii). Of course, many have gone to Southern California to do just that, and the culture, weather, and landscape seem somehow to encourage this kind of narcissistic endeavor. Many of his friends claimed that Hollywood ruined his writing, that work in the film studios and life in the continuous sunshine took the edge off his talent, and he did, indeed, wrestle with writer's block. However, Isherwood—who always had been a voluntary exile, detached from his surroundings, a camera—learned in the United States to live "intentionally," to invest himself in a purpose, to engage intimately with others, and to create a home. His new approach to life and living resulted in quite obviously different writing from that of the Berlin years. His earlier narrators were objective observers, dispassionate and wryly amused, their homosexuality inadmissible and veiled. Although it took Isherwood some time (and indeed some time for the culture to catch up to him), his narrators from his American period, especially from his two masterpieces *Christopher and His Kind* and *A Single Man,* are openly homosexual, less arch, and committed to revealing their thoughts and motives. California allowed Isherwood to live intensely and openly, and this invariably would change his writing, for, as Bucknell states, writing "was the only way he could rigorously examine and try to understand his experience" (xxxv).

As Isherwood's longtime partner, Don Bachardy, told me in a recent conversation, Isherwood didn't think the letters to Kathleen would be of interest to anyone because he felt he held back too much in them: "They were written by the English 'Christopher.' In Los Angeles he was 'Chris.'" But because Isherwood spent the rest of his life writing various forms of autobiography, seeing and performing himself in various roles, the letters to his mother give us a compelling and engaging look at a thoroughly personal side of Isherwood, a son writing to his mother. They are, as well, an intimate account of the private struggles of a writer and his circle as he tries to understand the larger, cultural violence of the middle decades of the twentieth century.

## WORKS CITED

Isherwood, Christopher. *Christopher and His Kind.* New York: Avon Books, 1976. Reprint, Minneapolis: University of Minnesota Press, 2001.

———. *Diaries: Volume One, 1939–1960.* Edited and introduced by Katherine Bucknell. London: Methuen, 1996.

———. *Kathleen and Frank: The Autobiography of a Family.* New York: Simon and Schuster, 1971.

Parker, Peter. *Isherwood: A Life.* London: Picador, 2004.

Phillips, Adam. Review of *The Lost Years: A Memoir, 1945–51. London Review of Books* 2, no. 22 (November 16, 2000): 6–8.

# *Acknowledgments*

Several years ago I was awarded a research fellowship from the Huntington Library to work with the papers of Christopher Isherwood for a book I was writing on British novelists in Hollywood, and it was then that I first came across the three boxes of letters from Isherwood to his mother and a cache of photographs that span most of Isherwood's life. Even though I was familiar with the events described in the letters, because Isherwood had narrated this part of his life in his own work, I was riveted by the vibrancy and humor, not to mention the urgency and drama, contained in them. I thought other readers of Isherwood, those who don't have the luxury of spending the summer in the graceful comfort of the Huntington Library's Manuscript Room, would appreciate the opportunity to read for themselves this fascinating correspondence and experience firsthand yet another Isherwood performance. Through the boundless generosity of Don Bachardy, this collection has been made available. It is impossible to say enough about the kindness, warmth, and enthusiasm of Don, who shares his time, his hospitality, and his energy so unselfishly with others. My deepest thanks and appreciation go to him for allowing me to reproduce the letters and for the opportunity to get to know him and his own amazing work.

I am equally indebted, grateful, thankful, indeed almost religious-feeling, about Sue Hodson, curator of manuscripts at the Huntington Library. Over the years, she has been a tireless friend and resource, and without her help and encouragement this book would not have been possible. Everyone at the Huntington has been a help and a delight, and my sincere thanks go to David Zeidberg, director of the library; Robert Ritchie, director of research; Romaine Ahlstrom, head of reader services; Mona Shulman, Susi Krasnoo, Christopher Adde, and everyone in reader services. Also, Edward Mendelson of the W. H. Auden estate was extremely helpful, charming, and generous, and I am grateful for his permission to reprint Auden's notes and letters.

Special thanks also go to Jim White, director of the Isherwood Foundation and a truly kind man who has been the soul of graciousness, patience, and generosity in making time for me in his always hectic schedule and answering even the most trivial of my questions. I am also grateful to James Berg, who was very helpful in finding a home for this book at the University of Minnesota Press, and Chris Freeman, wonderful scholars both and delightful friends, colleagues, and dining companions.

Thanks very much indeed to Douglas Armato, director of the University of Minnesota Press, and to Jason Weidemann. Not only do I deeply appreciate all of their hard work in reprinting lovely new editions of Isherwood's oeuvre, I also appreciate their enthusiasm in publishing this volume—not to mention their sense of humor. Thanks as well to Laura Westlund and to copy editor Mary Byers.

Additionally, I owe many thanks to Susan Chern and the Board of Research at Babson College for providing me with time and money to pursue and complete this project.

Last, but as far from least as one can imagine, my love and thanks to Stephen Croes, my inspiration, for all his love and support.

Kathleen *and*
Christopher

Emmastraat 24.

May 20.  **1935.**          Amsterdam.

My darling Mummy,

Thank you so much for your letter and for sending the money this morning. It safely arrived and our bills have been paid. I won't send you a cheque until my cheque arrives from America ( it must be here this week ) as I don't want the cash in the bank to get too low. This morning, H. and I went to the Police. H. proudly produced your registered envelope and was immediately given a permit to stay here three months. I, who could produce nothing, was told to come again at the end of June. But, of course, it'll be quite all right, as by that time I shall have an advice from the Westminster to cash my cheques at some bank here and shall be able to show that.

We have a very nice room, much nicer than in Bruxelles and not much more expensive. It costs 100 gulden a month, which is about £ 14. 10, with all meals included. And I hope to earn a little money by teaching. In fact, I've got two pupils in prospect already. We are also hiring a couple of old bicycles and so shall be able to go to the seaside, which is very close, whenever the weather is fine. Our landlady is an old friend : H. used to live with her when I was working at the film in England.

Yesterday, I fetched all the luggage from Bruxelles. Six pieces ! I shan't forget it in a hurry.

Best love,

C.

*I wish you a good time outside London. Kind regards, for you and Richard.*

*Heinz.*

# 1935

Isherwood and Heinz are living in Copenhagen in 1935, and in January W. H. Auden visits them in order to work with Isherwood on *The Dog beneath the Skin,* which is published by Faber and Faber in May. The Hogarth Press publishes *Mr Norris Changes Trains* and the U.S. edition (published with the title *The Last of Mr. Norris*) is published by William Morrow. Later in the year, Isherwood signs a new contract with Methuen and works on "A Berlin Diary" and "The Nowaks." As the political situation becomes increasingly disturbing—Hitler introduces conscription and Italy invades Ethiopia—Isherwood and Heinz move frequently in an effort to gain new citizenship for Heinz and keep him from having to return to Germany and register for the draft. They leave Copenhagen for Brussels and then go on to Amsterdam, where they take a flat next door to Klaus Mann, when Heinz receives a three-month permit to stay in Holland. The pair return to Brussels in the fall of the year and then in December move to Sintra, Portugal, where Stephen Spender and Tony Hyndman join them to set up housekeeping. In Portugal, Isherwood begins work on *Paul is Alone.*

January 2
Classensgade 65.
Copenhagen

My darling Mummy,

Thank you very much indeed for the lovely little calendar, which I got yesterday. It is so nice. I shall find it very useful, I'm sure.

Alas, the New Year hasn't opened very brightly for us here. We are involved in absurd new complications about our passports; so much so that it really seems doubtful if we shall be allowed to stay on here at all. Three days ago I had a long interview with the Police, who were charming but extremely suspicious. First of all, they wanted to know all about H. being obviously persuaded that I was secretly employing him.[1] I had to explain that famous alteration in his passport. Then they asked: But how is he living now? He can't be getting money from Germany, because no German living abroad can get more than 10 marks a month nowadays. So I explained that I was giving H. money, but added, to refute the employment theory, that this was simply an arrangement between my family and his and that you and his grandmother were acquainted. All this was received without much interest, but now they went on to cross-examine me about my own work. What did I write? Was it political: What were these translations I admitted to having made? Were they political? Etc, etc. Naturally, I firmly denied everything. Finally they said they would like to speak to any Danish friends I had. So today, our student friend, Paul Kryger, very kindly went and interviewed with them.[2] Unfortunately, he is also young, so didn't make a particularly weighty impression. Still, he did succeed in getting them to admit that the suspicions against me are mainly political. Isn't it fantastic? Especially as Denmark is crowded with self-confessed political emigrants of all kinds. Of course, I shall continue to protest and shall assemble the few witnesses to my respectability whom I have here, but I have a kind of feeling that it will do no good. Perhaps I have lost faith in ever again receiving justice at the hands of any officials, however polite. The Harwich incident has considerably soured me in that direction.[3] It is possible that the Spenders will be able to do something.[4] At present they're away.

The worst of it is, if we have to leave I don't know where we can go. Certainly, Sweden will be out of the question, as the Danish police would inform their colleagues, for certain. I feel hugely disgusted.

Last night we went to the opera and saw *Carmen,* which was very well done. Edward's new sketch has just arrived. It is awfully good, I think.[5]

Best love,
C.

February 7
Copenhagen

Would you be so kind as to ring up Durrants[6] (city 4963) and warn them that *Mr Norris*[7] is coming out soon and ask them to give notice in good time if my subscription runs short—as I don't want to miss any reviews. When the 5 copies come from Hogarth will you please keep one for yourself and ask R,[8] when he has time, to deliver the other four as follows: To Olive.[9] To Miss Balbernie (60 Redcliffe Gardens).[10]

To Roger Burford (Rickmansworth 487) whenever he or Stella is in town and calls for it.[11] To Hector, when he is back and can call for it.[12]

Best love,
C.

February 11
Copenhagen

My darling Mummy,

It seems a long time since I wrote to you, but nothing much has happened, I enclose a letter from Hugh Walpole which may interest you.[13] Please don't destroy it.

Thank R. for his letter. In it he asks me if I can advise him how Mrs Harpist is to "approach" a publisher about her novel. But there is really nothing to advise. Every decent publisher reads whatever is sent to him, as long as it is typed or legibly written: no influence or pulling of strings is needed. If it is a "real life" story, she might try Faber and Faber or Cape. If it has a socialistic twist, Martin Lawrence. She can deliver the manuscript by hand if she doesn't want to pay postage. It is very simple. I hope she knows that she is not, on any account, to mention my name. I have annoyed Cape's considerably already by sponsoring other peoples' manuscripts. And it's entirely unnecessary. If she has got into the B.B.C. premises, why doesn't she ask somebody there what they think? In the unlikely event of the novel being good, she won't have the least trouble placing it, I imagine.

Here, we skate but are sad. The future seems dark. The Danish authorities demand income-tax: a half year if we leave Denmark at the end of March, a whole year if we stay any longer. Sweden will be more expensive and Finland, which is cheap, seems very cold and far. Also, very soon, compulsory military service is being reintroduced in Germany. What is Heinz to do? If he goes back, he becomes part of the machine and won't be allowed out again for the next five years, perhaps longer. If he doesn't, he is an exile for the rest of Hitler's stay: and that may mean a lifetime. He is horrified at the thought of going: In Germany he has only his old grandmother, who will soon die, two married aunts and his father, who didn't bring him up and whom he never sees. If he stays with me, he must make some kind of life for himself. He wants to live in the country and keep animals (he is very good at that kind of thing) but where? All European countries are equally unfriendly to Germans and, in 1938, his passport will expire. He will have to get another nationality somehow, I suppose; but this is fearfully difficult and takes a great deal of time. I see more and more what a disaster that Harwich business was.[14] If only I could have got him into the country then and settled him down he might be well on his way to becoming English by now! Wystan[15] is going to make enquiries through Harold Nicolson[16] as to how bad a mark, if any, stands against his name on the records. But I doubt whether there's anything to be done in that direction.

The other alternative seems to be S. Africa; if I could ever get him in. I think about it all, over and over, and feel furious, but it's no good being angry: one is simply up against the system. If you aren't extremely cunning it destroys you. It is no good crying for sympathy. I suppose I shall find a way out of this somehow.

Best love,
C.

February 26
Classensgade 65.
København

My darling mummy,

Many thanks for your letter and for sending the parcel of papers, which arrived this morning. Everything is in order.

Yesterday I got a cheque £ 17. 5. 3: all that the income tax and Curtis Brown left out of twenty-five.[17] The income-tax I shall try and claim back later: the government refuse to spend it on the Unemployed anyhow, and I don't see why I should help pay for their aeroplanes and poison gas. Enclosed is a cheque for £ 15. 0. 0 (under sixteen pounds as Uncle H. would add);[18] the rest you shall have when the American firm pays up.

So far I have seen one notice of *Mr N.* in the *Telegraph*: very good, as far as it goes. No others. It was a great misfortune that Walpole didn't do anything about the Book Society because he was ill, as he says in his letter. I suspect Hogarth Press never bothered to submit another copy to the Society itself, at all.

I have written to the *Daily T.* pointing out the error: that *Mr Norris* had previously appeared in *The Memorial*. But this is also H. Ps [Hogarth Press] fault, calling the book "a successor" to *The Memorial*. I think the jacket is horrible. So stupid and cheap, as if my attitude to the Hammer and Sickle were "just another racket" like the books, the money, the swastika and the whip.

Hector is in London, staying with his mother.[19] Flat 2. 62 Greencroft Gardens. N.W. 6. If you could find the time to send him a card, he'll call for the book. My godson is due to appear on Thursday or thereabouts.[20]

The play I have written with Wystan is called *Where is Francis?*.[21]

It is about a young man and a dog who go out to hunt for the missing son of the village squire, who is called Sir Francis Crewe. This is just an excuse for a symbolic tour of fascist Europe. The heir turns out to be the Dog in disguise. I mean, the Dog turns out to be heir. I'll let you know all the details later. Anyhow, it's not impossible that I won't pay a short visit to London within the next two months. It all depends on where we go after Copenhagen.

Lately, I have been seriously thinking of emigrating to South Africa! Of course, it's out of the question till we raise some money; but at least it would be a life of some sorts, not a man-hunt as at present, and I could return to England "on leave". S. Africa is undoubtedly the best Dominion for Germans, and H. might gradually turn into a Boer and from a Boer into a Briton. Also, if we had a couple of acres of land there and a cottage, it could be in his name and would give him a kind of status. And he would be able to do the kind of work he wants. Even his father now frankly advises him not to return; so his conscience is becoming easier on the subject. Another visitor from Germany looked in on us today. Berlin seems to have become about as interesting as Burton-on-Trent. Everybody agrees that Hitler is there to stay. But I suppose they used say that about Napoleon.

Yes, I fear the P.O. war savings certificate was cancelled all right. If you ever have time, you might be so kind as to enquire.

Have heard nothing from Stephen for ages.[22] So glad R. is back at the farm.


                              Best love,
                              Christopher

                              many greetings
                              Heinz

March 12
Copenhagen

My darling Mummy,

Thank you very much for sending the cuttings book: also for
your letter and the new reviews which arrived this morning. *Mr N.* is
certainly getting more appreciation than *The Memorial,* though I can't
say I find any of the critics particularly intelligent in their remarks: I am
much shocked at the callousness with which they all completely ignore
the tragedy at the end. They seem to find German politics just one long
laugh. But I suppose that is my fault for not rubbing the reader's nose
in Bayer's and the Baron's blood, not to mention poor Otto.

How curious of Henry not to like the book. I mean, how untrue
to type.[23] Because I'd felt certain that it was just the Dickens aspect of
Mr Norris which *would* have appealed to him. Indeed, I feel that Mr
Norris, far from being "modern" in conception, is almost *too* faithful to
the English Comic Tradition which one gets so sick of hearing about.
He is merely a modernised Dickens or Smollett character. And this is
obviously what pleased Compton Mackenzie.[24]

Another psychological surprise is the attitude of Mr Norris himself.[25] Now that the book is out, he has forgotten all feelings of injury,
eagerly searches the press for reviews and notes successes with proprie-
tary pride: "We got a very good notice in the *Telegraph*" etc! It is he
whom I am going to visit in Belgium. If all goes according to plan, I
shall dump Heinz there and come across to England for a short visit
towards the end of April, staying, if possible, until the production of
*Where is Francis?*

I don't know yet when the Wintle christening will take place,
but I suppose I ought to attend that too.[26] Did I give my christening
mug away to Thomas? I believe I did. But I still have somewhere a cup

I won at St Edmund's in the Sports? The Wintle kid might have that? Or do you object? If you do, of course, I won't do anything about it, and perhaps christening mugs are out of date now? You'll know this better than I.

Yesterday I got the following telegram: "Very glad indeed to meet the fascinating Mr Norris. Sincere congratulations. Viertel"[27] Nice of him wasn't it? He may help sell a few copies at Gaumont British.

Here, the weather is very mild and the sun is warm. We went to see the castle of Elsinore, which stands on the edge of the sea, looking across to Sweden.

I plan now to finish as quickly as possible "Berlin Diary", which is quite short and practically non-fiction. Then I hope to do a big novel dealing with refugees; jews and communists. I should like to include "The Landauers"[28] out of my original version and also work with Viertel and the film studios and move the action about from one city to another: London. Las Palmas. Copenhagen. But this is all very vague. I expect it will boil down to another "delightful little comedy", with not more than half a dozen deaths.

Why does Henry object to my nom-de-plume? Disgrace to the family or what? I do hope the next cash-payment isn't in danger? I must write to him, but what on earth shall I say?

Best love to all,
C.

Many greetings
Heinz

March 18
Copenhagen

My darling Mummy,

Thank you very much for your letter and the cuttings. As you say, *Mr N.* doesn't seem doing badly on the whole.

As you will imagine, we haven't passed an over-cheerful weekend. I was expecting this to happen, of course; but hoping it would be much later, when I'd had time to make some sort of plans. The question now is: what shall become of H.? As soon as he's been formally called up and has formally refused to return to that mad-house he becomes, of course, from the Nazi point of view, a criminal. That means that when, in 1938, his passport expires, he won't be able to get a new one. So, in the meanwhile, he must get another nationality; either by adoption or settling in some foreign country. Adoption would probably be easier, if one could find the right sort of people to undertake it. Failing that, some nationality which can be bought outright (I believe Swiss, but it's fabulously expensive). So you see, I have plenty to think about!

Meanwhile, like Sir John Simon, I shall probably not postpone my visit. At present, there seems nothing to do but sit tight.

Don't tire yourself too much with all this selling.

Best love,
C.

Best regards
Heinz

March 27
Classensgade 65.
Copenhagen


Many thanks for your letter and the cuttings. Especially for sending the tax details. Could you ring up Hogarth and ask in what paper did Hugh Walpole's criticism appear? Durrant's seems to have overlooked it (?)

I hope to come to London about the 25th of April—not Easter. The play isn't now being performed till June, so it's no good waiting for that. Have you heard anything from Hector? And have you unearthed a christening present?

*Mr Norris* is due to appear in America on May 8. And now I hear there are translation offers, as well—but know no details.


Best love
C.


April 4
Classensgade 65.
København


Many thanks for your letter and the cuttings. We now expect definitely to leave here on the 13th, for Belgium. I shall probably go alone to Paris for Easter and cross to England from there on Easter Tuesday: but this isn't quite fixed. Don't worry about Mr N. I am not in the least bit involved. And it is no earthly use at this time of day pretending I don't know him![29] We shall stay on our own in an hotel.

I may send some parcels addressed to myself, to reduce our luggage: so you'll know what they are. If it would amuse you to talk to Michael Spender's wife about us, she is at S's flat: 25 Randolph Crescent. But I don't think you'd like her, much! She speaks good English.

Best love,
C.

April 11

Many thanks for your letter and the cutting. Could you send a photograph of me to the American publishers: William Morrow & Company 386 Fourth Avenue, New York? Better send the very ugly full face one where I haven't shaved, which Stephen took of me out of doors, in Berlin—because I think there are duplicates. You'll find it in my photo drawer, in the smoking room bureau.

An awful rush, packing here.

I've just had a letter from Paris which more or less forces me to put off coming to England until the *30th* of April. I am sorry to keep changing your plans but it is important. I will tell you all about it when we meet.

Best love,
C.

May 13
Bruxelles

Safely arrived, after a very rough crossing. All well here—except
that it appears H. must go to a Belgian Consulate *abroad* to get his
permit renewed. So we are making an excursion to Rotterdam either
Wednesday or Thursday! I think it will be all right. In any case, we shall
only stay the day. So much enjoyed my visit.

Love to all,
C.

Dear Mrs. Isherwood! Thank you very much for the nice stock-
ings. It was a great surprise for me. Best regards for you and Richard.
[Heinz]

May 20
Emmastraat 24.
Amsterdam

My darling Mummy,
Thank you so much for sending the money this morning. It safely
arrived and our bills have been paid. I won't send you a cheque until
my cheque arrives from America (it must be here this week) as I don't
want the cash in the bank to get too low. This morning, H. and I went
to the Police. H. proudly produced your registered envelope and was
immediately given a permit to stay here three months. I, who could
produce nothing, was told to come again at the end of June. But, of
course, it'll be quite all right, as by that time I shall have an advice from

the Westminster to cash my cheques at some bank here and shall be able to show that.

We have a very nice room, much nicer than in Bruxelles and not much more expensive. It costs 100 gulden a month, which is about £ 14. 10, with all meals included. And I hope to earn a little money by teaching. In fact, I've got two pupils in prospect already. We are also hiring a couple of old bicycles and so shall be able to go to the seaside, which is very close, whenever the weather is fine. Our landlady is an old friend: H. used to live with her when I was working at the film in England.

Yesterday, I fetched all the luggage from Bruxelles. Six pieces! I shan't forget it in a hurry.

Best love,
C.

I wish you a good time outside London. Kind regards for you and Richard.

Heinz.

May 28
Emmastraat 24.
Amsterdam

My darling Mummy,

It seems a long time since I wrote to you. I hope that, by now, you will be enjoying yourself in the country. You certainly have the right weather for it, if it is as fine as here. We seem to have got summer at last.

The mystery of Alice Szant is partially explained. A rather hysterical friend of mine in Berlin wrote to me the other day (and says he's writing to you too, to apologize) confessing that, in a "moment of frenzy" he'd decided to ring you up. Alice Szant is his girl friend. It seems that, when connection with London was finally established, he was so overcome that he couldn't speak himself. I still don't know what has happened to put him into such a taking, but such things are possible in Berlin, nowadays. Anyhow, the message wasn't, in any sense, a trick or a trap.

We are very well and doing quite a lot of cycling. The other day we rode out to Zandfoort, on the North Sea, and bathed. A wonderful beach, stretching for miles. We couldn't have done this in Bruxelles. I have got two pupils for lessons and there seems a prospect of more or less continuous reviewing for the *Listener*.[30] Ackerley liked my review of *A Parson's Daughter* very much and has already sent me another book, on Louisa Alcott. A third is arriving in a day or two. So I hope and think that, with due economy, we can avoid further debts, even in this expensive town. This month, what with England, the sudden move and all the expenses it brought with it, we shall have spent sixty pounds!

I think also that I shall get to know some nice people here. But, unfortunately, Klaus Mann isn't coming back till the end of July.[31]

I still hope to pop over later to see you.

C.

June 3
Emmastraat 24.
Amsterdam

My darling Mummy,

Many thanks for your letter with the enclosures. I am sending you at last the cheque for £ 40. with many thanks. I got a cheque for £ 43. from America, as it seems that, as a British author resident more than six months of the year abroad, I am not liable to British tax on money earned abroad. This is nice; as the American Tax is very low, only 4%.

I have also had a provisional offer to have the book translated into French. Also a vague letter from Gaumont British: would I like to discuss working for them again? I replied encouragingly but have heard no more so far.

So glad you are having a nice time. I am just back from an amusing week-end in Bruxelles. At Norris' invitation and expense. A rough draft of his book has turned up among old papers, so we can begin work soon.[32] We went to the exhibition, which is lovely at night, with illuminated fountains, and the pavilions on the whole much less vulgar than Wembley. At a final lunch, the conversation turned to the capitalist system and Arthur, talking French to a Swedish millionaire, produced the memorable declaration: "Je protests, mais j'en profite."[33]

Would you, when you get to London, order me a copy of T. E. Lawrence's *Seven Pillars of Wisdom,* which I see they are publishing very shortly. It costs thirty shillings. I have, however, a copy of his abridgement: *Revolt in the Desert,* which is now declared forever unobtainable; so probably this could be sold to a second-hand bookseller to defray expenses, when R. is in London again and has time.

Would you also then ask how my account stands? I wrote to the Bank once about it, but no reply.

> Best love,
> Christopher ~~Isherwood~~

(I mixed you up with the Bank!)

My best love to all Monkhouses.[34] I have now done 3 reviews—*Parson's Daughter*—Alcott (which I'll send you (the book I mean)) and *Hashish,* by Henry de Monfreid. None of these have so far appeared. This week, I hope.


June 8
Emmastraat 24.
Amsterdam

My darling Mummy,
    Thank you very much for your letter and for sending the War Stock warrant. I return it, signed. Perhaps, as you're going to the Bank anyhow, you'll be kind enough to pay it in for me? I also enclose one of my reviews for the *Listener,* in proof. They aren't very quick publishing them; but yesterday I got a letter from Ackerley saying that he liked all three of them very much and that *The Parson's Daughter* one is appearing in the next issue of the *Listener.* Would you please, whenever there is a review by me, send me an extra copy on Wednesday? Then it will arrive on Thursday. *Listeners* are otherwise, for some mysterious reason, not obtainable here until late Friday. As a general rule, I don't get it; but

should like the copies in which my reviews appear. Ackerley is sending me another book at once: T. S. Eliot's verse drama about Thomas a Becket, called: *Murder in the Cathedral.* I will send off the Louisa Alcott book within the next few days. Until Tuesday, it seems, the post offices are shut for parcels.

No, I never received any registered letter from Curtis Brown. But perhaps Nanny confused this with a registered letter from Paul Kryger from Copenhagen. If not, I must enquire.[35]

Have the free copies of *The Dog beneath the Skin* arrived yet? Faber and Faber are really the limit in casualness. I am getting very angry with them. I have written already.

About the proposed deed of allowance, I doubt if Henry would ever consent to it. Thirty pounds or no thirty pounds, he would feel that this definitely committed him. And surely I should have to pay income tax? But it's worth trying, certainly; as long as it's made quite clear that the idea comes from Symonds.[36] Henry could so easily think to himself: the best way of saving that thirty pounds is not to pay Christopher anything at all!

Sorry Wyberslegh was a bit of a disappointment.[37] It certainly is the most wretched weather. Here, too. Following on Copenhagen, I feel as if we'd had nine months of winter.

Poor Arthur was told, by one of the most distinguished specialists in Europe, that his heart is in a very bad way. He was ordered to give up coffee, wine and numerous little pleasures. He is terribly depressed. I think he will come here soon and write his memoirs.

Alas, the Gaumont people wrote, saying that the job they'd had in mind was something to be done in a rush, and it was too late. They promised to let me know if anything else turned up, etc.

No news, as yet, from U.S.A. about my novel.

H's father is now playing a lone hand in the conscription problem, somewhat to our alarm. In his eagerness to prevent H. being called up, he has written to the war office and applied for H. to be given extra leave to stay abroad. If nobody had said anything, the war office would most probably have forgotten all about H: now, there may well be trouble. However, it can no doubt be dealt with; as where there's a will there's usually also an itching palm.

We had a nice bicycle ride yesterday out to Edam. But it's too windy to get far.

Don't buy a copy of *The Dog beneath the Skin* until you hear from me, as, if I get four or more, you shall have one. One I must give to Balbernie, as she can't afford a copy. And one to Arthur in return for all his hospitality. And one I want to keep here, for business reasons. So if you get the copies, please open them and extract one for yourself and one for Balbernie. If there's a fifth, Olive must have it, provided Wystan hasn't given her one himself. A sixth should go to Viertel, if still in England.[38]

Best love.
C.

Best greetings, Heinz.

*[Written by hand at the top of the page:]*
on second thoughts, you'd better keep the 9/2d voucher for yourself—to cover postal expenses. If I don't owe you that much already?

June 16
Emmastraat 24.
Amsterdam

My darling Mummy,

Thank you for your card and letter and for sending the *Listener*
and ordering *The Seven Pillars*, etc. My *Revolt in the Desert* is not a first
edition, I'm afraid. Still, it may fetch something. The Oxford University
Press are soon reprinting Lawrence's translation of the *Odessy* (spelt
wrong). I should like that, too: but there won't be much rush for it, so
can order later. The N.Y. reviews not bad on the whole, I thought? The
press seems determined to ignore our play—but I see from the *Observer*
this morning that we head the best sellers, so there are some people
somewhere who are interested! What Curtis Brown had sent me was a
contract with Wystan to share all profits. C. B. have somehow got their
noses in on this: but anyhow it's convenient to have the cash paid automatically and divided between us. C. B. also write that Chapman &
Hall have offered £150 down for *each* of my next 3 novels—with large
royalties to follow. But Brown advises not closing with them—as Cape,
Heinemann, Peter Davies and Methuen are also on the track. I seem
suddenly to have become quite popular! And now all that remains is
to write a wonderful witty amazing amusing masterpiece to sell them!
C. Brown are so excited that they seem quite to have overlooked this
fact. Humphrey Spender is here for the week-end, en route for Austria,
which is nice.[39] He was in Tetuan and Xauen, too—so we could compare photographs and notes. He has the Morocco pictures fairly regu-
larly in *The Daily Mirror,* this coming week. On Saturday there was one
almost exactly like ours. I have now reviewed T. S. Eliot's *Murder in the
Cathedral* and shall soon proceed to William McFee's *Sailor's Wisdom.*
(Alcott and *Hashish* are also due to appear). Could you get me *The*

*London Mercury* for July when it comes out? It has a very remarkable story by Stephen in it. The Henry suggestion is clearly no good.

Best love
C.

Best greetings, Heinz.

—I forgot to tell you that we went to a concert the other evening— to hear Beethoven's Eighth and Ninth Symphonies. The concerts are extremely good, but very expensive. No seats under 3 gulden. We both enjoyed it very much.

June 21
Emmastraat 24.
Amsterdam

My darling Mummy,
Many thanks for your letter of this morning, with cuttings— as well as your other communications. They all seem a bit shy of the *Dog beneath the Skin*. But I think that Wystan and I, between us, have quite a public; so we shall probably sell, whatever the newspapers say. Unfortunately, the costs of Wystan's air-trip to Copenhagen have to be paid off before we get any royalties!
I continue to be busy. After much hesitation I wrote to the *Listener* and told Ackerley that *Sailor's Wisdom* by William McFee was so poor I didn't want to review it. So now there are only Alcott and *Murder in the Cathedral* waiting to appear. I got £ 1. 11. 6 for *Parson's*

*Daughter,* which was only 300 words. The other 3 are 500. Ackerley originally told me they pay £ 3. 3. 0 per 1000 words—so I wasn't expecting so much. But perhaps I shall only get the same for the 500 word ones. All this interests me considerably—as we have again £ 15 debts! It seems impossible to live for less than £35 a month together in this expensive country. However, I have another iron in the fire— a little story about some people we met on Hierro, in the Canary Islands.[40] If the *Listener* takes that (they have asked me to send a story) I shan't do so badly.

Also, yesterday, I started at last on my new novel. I hope it is going to be really good—not so superficial as *Norris* and yet in its own way funnier. The hero is a sort of van der Lubbe—an embodiment of madness and hysteria of our time. He is the type of ideal Liar, who no longer has the least notion that he isn't telling the truth. I think I can make him rather heroic.[41]

It was nice having Humphrey Spender here. He took a lot of photographs. Now, next week, John Lehmann is probably coming—on his way to England.[42] And Arthur is due to arrive on the first of July— for a month—to do the memoir book. Robson-Scott may also be coming about the middle of July.[43]

Plans are very vague. Heinz's father's efforts to compromise us may at any moment bear fruit: but, even if they do, I hardly suppose that it will alter things much. It only means, more and more definitely, that we must leave Europe. I have written to Lawrence to enquire about S. Africa. He is thoroughly established in Johannesburg now.[44] There is also Katz, going to Buenos Aires.[45] But nothing need be decided immediately. I'm not sure when I shall come to England. Perhaps in September, perhaps sooner: but hardly, I think, next month. How would it be if *you* came *here*? Or would you find it embarrassing? It might amuse you, in August, say, for a day or two. You would certainly see more of me than you do when I come to London: and Amsterdam is really very attractive. Think it over. Perhaps R—after his successful Marple trip—could be induced to come too?[46]

We have had torrents of rain all last week, but today is glorious and very warm. Heinz is taking our bicycles to pieces and cleaning them. I expect we shall be bathing in a day or two.

> Best love,
> C.
> Love to R and N.

June 28
Emmastraat 24.
Amsterdam

My darling Mummy,

Very many thanks for your letter, just arrived. I am so glad that you may consider coming here in August. And, of course, if R comes, it will be even nicer—though, as you say, I doubt if he will.

No, thanks, it's no use sending *The Observer*—I get it so easily. I have now 3 reviews waiting to be printed: Alcott, *Odd Man Out* by Douglas Goldring and *Waiting for Nothing* by Tom Kromer. There is another, I haven't yet finished. The *Listener* paid £ 2. 12. 6 for *Hashish*, which was quite decent of them. It is very kind of you to offer to pay £ 10 of my debts—but I think we'll leave it, thank you, until I see how I come through in the long run. The *Listener* has accepted my story, but it may not be printed till August.[47] Could you, while I remember, send me a shilling's worth of 2d stamps—to stick on cheques?

Poor Bill Lichtenberg had the most extraordinary death.[48] He was experimenting with picture varnish and something he was heating exploded, burning him, not badly. He went to bed, seeming in little pain, and next day was quite cheerful. Then he slowly became unconscious and died in 48 hours. It seems that the burnt tissues had poisoned his whole system. Olive will tell you more about it. I heard from her.

No, there are no public meals here. We eat in our rooms. On July 1 we are moving into a much better room on the top floor at the same price. The landlady is a German who married a Dutchman. She speaks English.

Must finish in haste as H. and I are going to bicycle to Alkmaar to see the cheese market. Terrific heat the last few days.

Best love,
C.

Heard from Hector. Baby well, but not yet christened.[49] Wrote asking what I should give. A novel by him* about the Far East will be published by Duckworth in the autumn! And *Edgar* perhaps also (expurgated) later.

*Hector, not the baby!

July 1
Amsterdam

Could you, if the heat isn't too great ask R to get a copy of *Mr Norris* from Hogarth and send it to:

Frau Alice Van Nahuys
Riva Bella
Brissago bei Locarno
Tessino Switzerland

I want to pay for the copy and on no account must there be a bill in the parcel. If the Hogarth send it, they're sure to send a bill—such idiots.

She's a publisher here whom I know.

Also, could you ring up Temple Bar 1873 (Curtis Brown) ask to speak to Mr David Higham[50] and ask him why on earth he hasn't sent my copy of my agreement with Wystan for *Dogskin*. Also, why he hasn't answered my letter with other questions. He is getting awfully casual.

Terrific heat. We had a nice bike ride yesterday.

Just finished another review: *Devon Holiday* by Henry Williamson.

Best love,
C.

July 6
Amsterdam

My darling Mummy,

Many thanks for your letter and the cuttings. Would you mind sending me a copy of the *Criterion,* if it's not more than a shilling? For one thing, Durrants have only sent me cuttings which would have to be stuck double-sided on to a page—if you understand what I mean! And also it is perhaps a possible market for short sketches. I hope to do several of these from time to time; as the one which will appear in the *Listener* seemed to please Ackerley, and isn't too bad, I think. Ackerley has been most decent: he says he can't send me very many books as he has such hundreds of reviewers. But he favours me grossly, all the same, and pays more than the usual rate. And now he's going round trying to canvass other editors to give me reviewing, as well. I've also had the offer of some translating, from Geoffrey Bles.[51] Nothing definite, as yet. But there's quite a lot of money in it. I met him the other day in Amsterdam: rather a stupid man, but a great *Norris* fan!

The news about Henry is *too awful*!! Particularly as I don't know how on earth to entertain him.[52] Poor Heinz won't be at all his line I'm afraid. If only we were in Brussels, I could take him out in the evenings to the night-life. But here there isn't any! Anyhow, it will quite spoil your visit. Let's hope he won't come. Couldn't you announce that you weren't going, for some reason? And then come secretly? Anyhow, it won't be till the second half of August, as Mr Norris must first complete his month here, on the book. And on the 18th, H. must get his permit to stay here renewed: always a business.

Very interested to hear about *England Made Me*. I always feel that Graham and I are very similar writers; but I think he is far too arty.[53] The lavatories are probably due to his being a catholic and all in a mess. I don't believe that a young man nowadays can be a catholic and a serious writer at the same time. There are too many conflicting interests at work. The lavatories are the result of the conflict. It is exactly the same as the roses and the moonlit lake which a Victorian writer would have fallen back on when confronted with a difficulty he couldn't solve. All the same: *It's a Battlefield* is one of the most interesting failures I have read.

John Lehmann is billed to arrive this afternoon.

Best love,
C.

July 30
Emmastraat 24.
Amsterdam

My darling Mummy,

Thank you for your card and for sending the various papers, etc. Also, for getting the two copies of *The Memorial*. Of course, Hogarth have absolutely no right to demand the full price for the books: tell them so, please. If they make a fuss, I'll write to them myself. In any case, I'm quite glad of the chance of having a row with them as this will make my exit easier. I have now received offers from the other publishers which make it certain that I must go elsewhere. Heinemann would advance £ 75 for my next book; Peter Davies would advance £ 100 for each of my three next novels; Cape ditto; Chapman & Hall £ 150 for the next three; Methuen £ 300! I am at present trying to find out if I can extract anything from Methuen before I have written anything at all! If so, they win.

Higham is incredibly slack about answering letters and Miss Chapter of the Foreign Dept simply doesn't write at all. You and Richard really do everything for me which an agent ought to do.

Yes, I read the article in the *Listener*. It is flattering to be taken as an example; but I think the article itself was very unjust and silly. All it amounts to is that my sort of propaganda is implicit and the other peoples' is crude and superficial.

Mr Norris is back in Belgium, working with the powers of darkness to get H. a permit to return there; so perhaps your visit will be to Belgium after all. But I doubt it. I work spasmodically on his book. Have also received three books from the *New Statesman*. They will be altogether in one article, over my name. Just finished another book for the *Listener*, called *Sing Sing Doctor*, very gruesome, with descriptions of the electric chair, etc.

It seems that H. has very bad eyesight and should wear glasses. However, we're doing nothing about it for the present.

Horrible weather here, rain most of the day. I have just heard from the Dutch publishers that they aren't going to do *Mr Norris,* as they think it "too topical". But they *say* they're going to order a copy of *The Memorial* and read that.

Arthur keeps sending postcards under different names to the Albatross company recommending *Mr Norris.* He has sent forty already!

Best love,
C.

*[Written at top of page:]* Forster and Stephen visit us at the end of the month. Wystan may be flying to Australia to make a G.P.O. film! Is the *In Search of History* yours? Would like to read it. No thank you. Have already seen Forster's review.[54]

August 6
Amsterdam

My darling Mummy,

*The 7 Pillars* arrived at last this morning. Very many thanks. At present, we are waiting to hear the result of a new attempt by Arthur to get H. permission to reside in Belgium. But, in any case, I think the 19th would be a good date for your visit. *Should* things go un-expectedly quick and we be able to move that date, then you'd come to Belgium instead.

Arthur will almost certainly be in Norway just then!

I see no reason why you shouldn't stay here—except for the German boy, Toni, who is becoming rather a bore. He talks very good Bond St. English and drinks. I wish his friend would arrive and take him away.[55]

Will write again soon. Have received an offer from Cape to reprint my translation of Baudelaire's *Journals*! Also a club in Nottingham wants to perform *Dogskin* in January. The Dutch publishers have refused *Norris*. So far done nothing about Curtis Brown. But think I'll stick by them. Higham is almost certainly a crook—worse: a stupid crook.

Will write again soon. Robson-Scott here for one night. Heinz well. Arthur and I busy on the book, with short hand typists.

Best love, also to R and N.
C.

Best greetings, Heinz

August 12
Amsterdam

No fixed plans as Belgium hangs fire still, but we can't wait any longer. I suggest you arrive here on Sunday next, the 18th and stay till the 23rd. That makes four clear days: Forster with friends is turning up on the 24th: but the whole of your stay will be undisturbed. Mr N. leaves for Belgium tomorrow. I hope to get you a room here, but anyhow will find one. With luck, the German boy will also have been removed—plans are on foot.

Only don't get your ticket till the last moment, as we might make a sudden dash to Belgium and receive you there, instead. In any case, if you can come, I regard the visit as a fixture—it shall take place somewhere.

Best love in great haste,
C.

And will you send Heinz Neddermeyer £ 30 at once in a registered letter to this address? You might enclose a short note: Dear Heinz, I am sending you your allowance, as usual. I hope you are well. Many Greetings.

Needless to say, the money will be waiting for you on your arrival!

August 29
Amsterdam

My darling Mummy,

Thank you very much indeed for your letter and birthday presents—the handkerchiefs and the photograph. The handkerchiefs will come in most usefully. Thank you also again for the other books you have given me. And thank you for your visit, which was a great pleasure. I'm so glad you enjoyed it, too.

I should have written before this; but the days have been very busy ones. On Saturday, Brian Howard and Toni returned from England by air, having been shown the door at Croydon![56] So they were in a terrible state and also enraged because the Dutch Air Line demanded payment for the return flight. And Toni had had to spend the night in a police station! Really, one talks about the Captain Kane case and the brutality of Spanish justice, but it would be difficult to find anything more primitive, idiotic, and calculated to make tourists determined never to set foot in our country. Brian said that even a respectable middle-aged American couple were treated with the utmost rudeness and only given a fortnight's permission. I begin to feel that we really got off quite lightly at Harwich!

Saturday also came Forster and his friend Buckingham and we went straight off that afternoon to Zandvoort and bathed: a good thing we did as that was the last of the fine weather.[57] Today it is thundery with heavy showers and much cooler. On Monday, Stephen arrived unexpectedly and we went to the Isle of Marken for the afternoon. On Tuesday, we went to the Hague, where we met Gerald, Klaus came too, as well as Brian and Toni, and everything was set for a really nice birthday party, but the rain came in torrents and we had to come home early.[58] However I enjoyed myself greatly. Gerald left for Norway yesterday from Rotterdam. He will return on the 8th. Meanwhile there are still hopes of Belgium; of which I will tell you more if they seem to be materialising. So we shall stay for the present. Stephen will probably stay till Sunday. Forster and Buckingham left this morning. We all enjoyed ourselves greatly. Forster says he will ring you up and tell you about it.

Brian and Toni, continue, of course, to wait here for news of the Irish scheme. Klaus Mann also leaves today. He is going to Persia, via U.S.S.R. Cape's write that, after all, they won't publish the Baudelaire translation: I think Eliot put them off it. In the *Listener* this week is my little sketch: "The Turn Round the World." Katz writes that he doesn't anticipate a European war at present, which is cheering.

Could you ask Hogarth how *Mr Norris* is going?

Best love and many thanks,
C.

Kind regards, Heinz

September 19
Bruxelles

Well, we're here and already installed in the most amusing flat
you ever saw. Full of photographs of film-stars and . . . cake-trays and
large silk dolls. There is a kitchen and (in the bedroom) a very beautiful
bath. Our landlady makes our breakfast, cleans our rooms and washes
our clothes—all without charge! She has certain resemblances to Frl.
Thurau.[59] The flat costs 800 Belgian francs a month, with light and gas
(£ 1 = 145). Gerald also has a very nice flat—but ours is more central—
right in the middle of the town. I signed the contract with Methuen
today.

> Best love,
> C.

> Also to R, if you're with him.

September 21
chez Madame Markle
Boulevard Adolphe Max 22.
Bruxelles

My darling Mummy,
Very many thanks for your letter and for enclosing the card from
Weyland.[60] I suppose you won't have understood it? He very tiresomely
asks for the return of his manuscripts—tiresomely, because, as ill-luck
would have it, I sent them in my last parcel of papers to Pembroke

Gardens. Perhaps as soon as you return, you'll be kind enough to let me have them? They're in two envelopes, both addressed to me in Copenhagen: typescript in German, on thin paper. One of the manuscripts has a title page on which my name occurs. (Or, on second thoughts, I believe I destroyed this; not wishing it to go through the post, as it's political propaganda.)

I got a letter from Curtis Brown the other day with the contract from Methuen. I signed it. As soon as the signed counterpart is returned to me, I get a cheque for £ 150 (less tax, etc); the other £ 150 will be paid on publication of my book. Now that this money is more or less guaranteed, I wonder if you could lend me £ 200 or even, if you could manage it, £ 300? I should like to have the money and put it into safe-deposit here, in case we have to make any sudden moves. Not that I anticipate any, but the European situation is looking nasty and may well be worse by the time you receive this letter. If sanctions are applied, there may be a decree to prevent money being sent out of the country—you never know. So it's best to be prepared. As long as things don't look too bad, we shall keep to our plan of trying to get permission to stay here. It is very nice indeed in this flat and our landlady is really a jewel. I also should like to come to England in the near future. Alas, I hear from Olive that the play isn't being produced till the early Spring.

No, I haven't read Elizabeth Bowen, but I want to. Forster was praising her.

Some ghastly new books to review for the *Listener: Perilous Privilege* (dreary fuss about adolescence in Scottish Lowlands) and *Shark! Shark!* one of those haw-haw travels, "and believe me, the shark enjoys the hunt every bit as much as we do," or words to that effect.

No more now, I must take this out to the post.

Best love,
C.

Please give my love to Richard and remember me to the Monkhouses—if they seem kindly disposed.


September 25
Hotel Plaza Bruxelles

My darling Mummy,

Thank you very much for your letter, which arrived this morning. As regards the money, would you please send it to me at the Adolphe Max address? Registered—in notes? By the way, I quite understand that £ 300 is a lot of money—and £ 250 will do—but perhaps I didn't make it clear that I am repaying you £ 100 by cheque *immediately*? *If*, therefore, you *could* manage £ 300, I should be very grateful; but shall perfectly understand if you can't.

I am writing from the above address only because I am waiting for somebody in the lounge! We continue to be very pleased with our landlady and our flat. And I really believe that Heinz is going to get his permit extended. In any case, I am to go and interview with the man there tomorrow.

Very busy reviewing a book by Lindburgh's wife, called *North to the Orient*. Extremely good: you'd like it, I know.

Best love, also to Richard—
C.

Tuesday, December 10
Boulevard Adolphe Max 22
Brussels

My darling Mummy,

many thanks for your letter. Well, we are just off to Antwerp to
see about our boat. It sails either today or tomorrow early but we are
allowed to sleep on it tonight.[61] It is called the "Bage"—a Brazilian boat
going to Rio. We have first class cabins for eight pounds each. But I
think it is chiefly cargo and only takes a few passengers.

I enclose a sheet of the Week. Will you put it with the others in
the bureau drawer?

Don't be alarmed if you don't hear from us for a good long time;
as the voyage will be very leisurely! I think we shall stop at Harve, Vigo
and Oporto.

Best love,
C.

21st December 1935
Villa Alecrim do Norte
San Pedro, Sintra, Portugal

My darling Mummy,

Above is our new address. As you see, we have found a house
already—address above. We have taken it for three months, furnished,
while we look round for something really nice and learn Portuguese and
generally get used to the manners and customs of housekeeping in this

country. It belongs to an English lady who believes in reincarnation and
does nasty washy water-colours of flowers.[62] But she has furnished it
quite comfortably and each of us will have his own room, which ought
to make working easier. We also have a common room *and* a dining
room, so you see we shall be living in the greatest luxury! The house
costs £30 for three months. We have engaged, through the English
lady, two servants: the cook for 25 shillings a month and the maid for
rather under a pound. So you see, living is cheap here! Tony is going
to supervise the house-keeping and Heinz will keep hens and maybe
rabbits.[63] We have already bought a puppy, about the size of a large rat.
His name is Teddy. Last night he made six different messes in our bedroom. We move out of the hotel today and into the Villa Alecrim. The
weather is perfectly horrible, driving wind and rain. You would love this
place. It is a large village of tumbledown eighteenth century palaces and
one can quite imagine Byron coming here. You know he wrote some
stanzas about Sintra in *Childe Harold*? The village is built on a steep
hillside and our house will have a wonderful view right down the valley
to the sea. This valley, unlike the surrounding country, is very fertile
and full of sub-tropical trees and plans. The day we arrived, we drove
straight out in a taxi from Lisbon to Brian Howard's house, which is at
Collares, a little hamlet about eight kilometers from Sintra itself. The
house is a wonderful old ruined sixteenth century monastery in a huge
half-wild garden. The original gateway is still standing and you ring
a bell over the double gates which open into a little court-yard. The
chapel still exists but it has been used as a lumber room and the altar is
stacked with broken furniture. I think Brian would like to restore it and
to open up the disused wing but he only has the house on a very unsatisfactory lease which forces him to leave it for four months of every year
while the owner lives there.

Yesterday, we went into Lisbon and I found your card waiting for me at Cooks, From now on, they are going to forward everything to the villa, anyway. From the beginning of January, as you have probably discovered, there will be air service direct to Lisbon and you will be able to get letters through pretty quick if they are urgent. We are all very well and happy. Very best love and Christmas wishes to you and Richard. I am not sending any Christmas cards this year as everything is in such a muddle but please give my best love to Nanny and greeting to Elizabeth.[64]

Always your loving
Christopher

Christmas Greetings, Tony Hyndman
Best wishes for a happy Christmas
to you and to Richard—Stephen
Best Christmas greeting to both
of you. Heinz

Villa Alecrim.

April 8, 1936

My darling Mummy,

Thank you for your card and please forgive me ; I have been so very busy that I haven't had a moment for writing. The play is now ready in rough draft and half of it, the first of the two acts, is typed out ready for the publisher. It is interesting, I think : far more so than Dogskin and far more experimental, as it is an attempt to blend absolutely straight acting dialogue, rather reminiscent of Journey's End, with various kinds of verse dialogue. The theme is really the life of Col onel Lawrence, but set into a climbing expedition on a big tropical mountain. It will be called : The Ascent of F.6. Wystan will stay here about a fortnight more, by which time I hope to have the whole thing ready for him to take back. We are also going to do a school composition book together ; something quite new of its kind. I have also seven books waiting to be reviewed ! There is a great deal of minor news about local characters, but it will keep. So sorry your arm is bad. Yes, we have taken this house on for a year. Rather madly, considering that H. is now liable at any moment to be plunged into difficulties with his passport, and conscription, but one lives from week to week. The weather is turning fine at last, the hens are doing well and the baby rabbit thrives. When are you coming out here ? It would be fun if you could Nothing from the Hogarth Press. Forster is said to have got through his operation nicely. I have written to him, but no answer yet. He may visit us later. Glad you liked the review I felt rather disgusted with it. Very difficult to do one's friends. Stephen writes en route for Greece. Henry has sent the money. In a week or two, we hope to begin to bathe.

I will write again soon.

Best love,

C.

Thank R. for his wonderful letters. Love to N.

# *1936*

Auden and Isherwood's play *The Dog beneath the Skin* opens at the Westminster Theatre in London, and in the spring Auden goes to Portugal to work with Isherwood on *The Ascent of F6*, which is published later in the year by Faber and Faber. Despite domestic upheaval, Isherwood finishes a draft of "Sally Bowles" and works on *Lions and Shadows*. He decides to abandon *Paul is Alone* and returns to work on *The Lost*, which will eventually become *Goodbye to Berlin*. The living situation in Portugal is not ideal, and Spender and Hyndman go to Spain in support of the Republican cause and are there when civil war breaks out in July. Also in July, the government catches up with Heinz, and he is ordered by the German consul in Lisbon to report for military service, which he does not do. World events are escalating: Germany occupies the Rhineland early in the year, and later Franco is declared chief of state in Spain and Mussolini declares the Rome–Berlin axis. In England, George V dies in January and is succeeded by Edward VIII, who abdicates later in the year and is succeeded by his brother George VI.

[Lisbon]
January 2

Thank you so much for your letter and the little diary. I like yours much better than Kearsey's,[1] which I have given to Heinz. The mix-up about *The Jack and the Ell* and *The Last of Mr Norris* is that they are alternative titles—one merely suggested, the other actually used—for the U.S.A. edition of *Mr N. Changes Trains*. If you've told the book-sellers this, there's no need to add more. All well here. Will write again properly soon.

Best love,
C.


January 6
Villa Alecrim do Norte
Sao Pedro
Sintra.

My darling Mummy,

Thank you very much for your letters and cards. I'm afraid I wrote very briefly the other day from Lisbon. We had been shopping and I was awfully tired. The weather continues foul, but occasionally we have a wonderful morning or afternoon of sunshine, when it is quite as warm as May in England. Then we go for walks up the hill to the castle.

The view, even from my window, is superb. I can see fifteen or twenty miles as I sit writing this, right over the valley to the north of Sintra, to a low range of hills.

The next problem to be tackled is Heinz's passport. Unfortunately, he has to go to the German Consul to get a paper saying that his papers are in order. The Portuguese permission then follows automatically, more or less. But we are so afraid that the German Consul will say that H. must return at once to Germany for his military service, and he might take possession of his passport, which would leave us stranded. However, this ordeal is not to be faced until the end of February. Meanwhile we look around for a house with a big garden, where we can settle. There are certainly a great many to choose from. The dog and the hens are doing well. The rabbits arrive today or tomorrow. Later, we hope to have doves, ducks, a peacock, monkeys, cockatoos, etc.

Am very busy on my novel.[2] I think it is much the best thing I have done so far, if only I can pull it off. Very soon, I hope, my long sketch "The Kulaks" will appear—in the first number of John Lehmann's quarterly book (a sort of Yellow Book) which will either be called *New Writing* or *The Bridge*. "The Kulaks" is very directly written and not a bit arty, so I hope people will like it.[3] The *Listener* has now three reviews of mine to publish: *Proletarian Pilgrimage, Shark! Shark!* and *The Way of a Transgressor*. I am now grappling with Galsworthy's *Life and Letters*, a huge dreary book, because he couldn't write letters and hadn't any life. It is an awful pity it was ever written, I think; because Galsworthy is really quite a good writer and this book just makes one feel he was an old fool. He was essentially a narrator, a reporter, and yet he had this fatal leaning towards philosophising and making statements and theories. And as all the philosophy is the kind which might come from any thoroughly right-minded lawyer or doctor, it is just terribly dull. He is so awfully sane; whereas, if a novelist is to philosophise at all, he must be a bit dotty, like Tolstoy or D. H. Lawrence or

Hermann Melville. The great writers of novels who were sane—like James—had the sense to confine themselves to narrative.

Now I must stop as Stephen is taking this to the post.

Best love,
Christopher


January 18
Villa Alecrim do Norte
Sao Pedro
Sintra.


My darling Mummy,

Thank you very much for your letter, the programme and invaluable report of *Dogskin*.[4] So far only Olive has written and she only briefly.[5] I was most interested. But on the whole I think I'd rather have been present at your film debut: that sounds too thrilling for words. I do hope that I shall one day see the film itself. I think Olive was rather envious that she herself wasn't considered sufficiently "good of her kind" to appear! They informed her rather unkindly that she was declassed!

Miss Mitchell was much interested to hear of the coincidence about your neighbors: however I gather that they aren't in much favor with her because when I referred to them as "your friends" she replied hastily "don't call them my friends, please—they're my sister-in-law's friends, not mine."[6] Also, the suggestion about the milk started a feud of no mean proportions: our Miss Mitchell strenuously denies that there is anything wrong with the milk produced by our milkman: the other is an American and much disliked by the Portuguese! So we are sticking to the old. We now have a kitten, to add to the white rabbits, hens and dog. I don't know why Mrs Schuster assumed that we didn't want chickens: of course we do. And anyhow Tony holds strong views on the subject of animals being deprived of the society of the opposite sex!

We are getting deeper and deeper into the abyss of Sintra society. There is a Lady Carrick[7] and her companion who do astral drawings: pictures of the colour-values of Beethoven's Fifth Symphony and so forth. We are keeping a journal describing them which you shall see some day. Also a very nice young French poet and an attractive scandal-mongering lady named Mrs Norton who has a feud with the Mitchells. Humphrey is here.[8] He has just shaved off all his hair, so as to make it grow better, and now refuses to appear without a cap.

I have written to Mrs Monkhouse. Very sorry hear about old Allan, but expect they had all had enough of his illnesses, including himself. It must have been miserable.[9] Poor Forster has had an operation: did I tell you?[10] And now he must have another. It is wretched for him, painful and quite dangerous. It would be awful if he died: he stands for so much which is admirable and is so charming and kind: besides, he is quite a young man.

I think John Lehmann's *New Writing* is going to be very interesting indeed: he has got a lot of continental authors. Edward's first section of the *Border Line* appears in the first number.[11] You know, don't you, that *Dogskin* is being performed this week by the Philodrama Society at Nottingham? They are giving several performances. The part of Alan Norman is being taken by a girl, in the pantomime fashion! I'm not sure if this is a good idea or not. The new ending of *Dogskin* I haven't seen. That was my own laziness. I suppose Wystan ran it together at the last moment.

Well I must end now to catch the post,

best love,
C.

January 19
Villa Alecrim do Norte
Sao Pedro
Sintra, Portugal

My darling Mummy,

I wrote to you yesterday: this is just to enclose a letter for Wystan; would you please see that it reaches him and send me his address?

And would you please make enquiries about translations of Balzac into English?[12] The Everyman edition is a reprint of a uniform English edition of the whole of Balzac's works, edited by Prof. Saintsbury. They don't say who publishes this uniform edition or how big or how expensive it is, but do give a list. Now the volumes I want are:

*A Distinguished Provincial at Paris.*

(this is really part *two* of *Illusions Perdues* and is called: *un grand Homme de province à Paris.* It is *not* to be confused with *Illusions Perdues,* part *one,* which is published in the Everyman Edition under the title: *Lost Illusions.*)

*A Harlot's Progress*

(called in French: *Splendeurs et Misères des Courtisanes.*)

Of course, there may be other and better and cheaper translations of these books. I don't mind which translation it is or which edition, so long as it is complete and inexpensive. You must watch out specially for *Splendeurs et Misères* being complete, because it is the kind of book which might be bowdlerized. It is, I hasten to assure you, a perfectly respectable classic—you needn't feel the least ashamed at asking for it! I am developing a craze for Balzac: he would have been the man to do *Mr Norris* justice! But it's very difficult to read him in French, as he is so technical.

Best love,
Christopher

January 30
Villa Alecrim do Norte
Sao Pedro
Sintra.

My darling Mummy,

Thank you very much for your letter, for the *Observer,* which arrived this morning, and for making enquiries about Balzac. It is absolutely disgraceful that there should be no uniform edition of Balzac
in English: Bennett was quite right to make a fuss about it. However,
I dare say Lamley will be able to get the volumes I want second hand
fairly easily. Jack's five shillings will go towards paying you for them,
of course.[13] I will send you the balance when I know what it is. (I have
long since written to thank Jack for the money.) I'm afraid the performance of *Dogskin* is not well timed and suppose it is doomed to be a
flop. Anyhow, I am very sorry that Doone was ever allowed to give it
a public performance at all: and I should certainly have been shown
the revised scene.[14] I am well aware that Wystan was afraid to send it
to me because he thought I might object to it and he's scared to offend
Doone, who is very much the little prima donna. But I'm not really
cross with either of them: it's not important enough. But please let
Wystan know that I now wish to have the manuscript of the last scene
sent to me and the questions answered which I asked in the letter. He
wrote me an absurd note the other day, suggesting that I should come
to England for the performance—as though it were a trip down to
Southend.

We were all much interested by your account of the lying-in-state:
also by Graham's article, which I'm afraid I can't regard as anything but
the most nauseating hypocrisy.[15] I shall never feel quite the same respect
for him again—and in the *Daily Mail,* too! There are plenty of people

who can write that kind of thing and mean it, without Graham having to scramble in with the rest, all for the sake of a couple of guineas. For those of us who cannot sincerely feel bowed to the earth with sorrow the decent thing is to keep one's mouth shut. I consider that when a writer like Graham, who has written a book like *It's a Battlefield,* stoops to write such insincere trash as that article he is offering a personal insult to the royal family and to everybody who is really in mourning.

Would you please pay this cheque into my account? I have now three reviews due to appear: *Proletarian Pilgrimage,* Marrott's *Life of Galsworthy* (signed) and Sean O'Casey's *Five Irish Plays.* I have written to Curtis Brown, suggesting that they make Methuen extend my time limit until March 1937. I shall feel much happier if they do: I want lots of time to finish the novel.

Gerald is here for a few days.[16] The weather is a little better, but we have had the most miserable lot of rain. Heinz is very busy and happy with his animals. Today he is making a kennel for Teddy. One of the hens has started to lay. Tomorrow is Heinz's birthday. We shall be a party of the seven, including Anton Altmann.[17]

Please give my love to R. when you write.

Best love,
C.

And will you please send me some more 2d. stamps for cheques?

February 9
Villa Alecrim do Norte
Sao Pedro
Sintra.

My darling Mummy,

Thank you for your letter, card and all the cuttings. *Dogskin* seems to have done as well as can be expected. I hear from Curtis Brown that there is some chance of having a proper production in America.

I enclose a cheque, which will you please cash in? Also Durrants' bill. Will you please pay and renew? It is very kind of you to knock off £ 50 of my debt. It will be a great help because I may have to pay out a good big sum in rent if we take on this house for a year, as I dare say we well may. I see no alternative at present. We needn't decide until the end of this month.

Will you please ring up Curtis Brown (Temple Bar 1873) and ask to speak to Mr Spencer Curtis Brown. I have had a silly letter from him today, not answering any of my questions and despair of getting anything out of him verbally. Please tell him *I want quite definitely to ask* Methuen to extend my period for sending in my next novel until the middle of March 1937—that is to say, *an extension of six months.* He writes that he doesn't advise it because the public will have forgotten *Mr Norris.* But I didn't ask him for his advice, I gave him instructions to carry out. If I try to rush *Paul is Alone* it will merely be a flop, like *Dogskin.* I'll never rush anything again. As for the public, they will like it if it comes off, even if they have to wait ten years. I want a *written assurance direct from Methuen* about the time-limit as I don't trust them an inch.

Another thing I want to know from Curtis Brown, and which I asked him in vain in my letter, is when *I can hope to get some cash on*

*Dogskin,* either from *America* or *England.* By the way, Gerald's book has been refused on the ground that it's too libellous![18]

The weather is horrible again today, after two days of fine weather. The day before yesterday, we went to visit Mafra, one of the biggest baroque convents in the world, if not the biggest. It is absolutely superb, and if you ever come out here, as I hope you may, you must see it. It stands in a tiny village, miles from anywhere, and dominates the whole landscape. I think that in its own way it is quite as remarkable as the acropolis. The whole place is shabby but not in the least ruinous; in just the right romantic state of disrepair. There are wonderful Italian statues in the church (which is not much smaller than St. Paul's) and miles and miles of huge almost empty rooms. The royal apartments—like all royal apartments in Portugal   have an extraordinary charm, faded and touching, with some lovely Empire furniture, but everything very primitive, really. Their bathrooms were worse than the worst pensions I have ever lived in!

Gerald writes from Tangier that weather is marvellous there. We envy him. Stephen thinks of going off to Greece with Tony at the end of March. Heinz was delighted with the ten shillings. He has written to you. We have three hens laying, now!

Best love, also to R. and Nanny,
Christopher

February 20
Villa Alecrim do Norte
Sao Pedro
Sintra.


My darling Mummy,

Here is a very belated christmas card! It is a lino-cut of the old
summer palace at Sintra, done by Miss Mitchell. The curious cones
on the top of the building are the chimneys of the palace kitchen:
one of the most curious features of the whole place. I don't think this
is a masterpiece, but it gives you some idea of what the palace looks
like and you may care to have it. You can show it to your neighbours.
(Incidentally, I don't gather they ended up on very brilliant terms with
the Mitchells: there was some dispute about the rent.)

I think we shall get the permit all right, but now the Nazis have
published a new decree that all Germans living abroad must report for
conscription, so there is another problem to deal with. Steps of various lengths could be taken. It is just a question of how and when and
which.

Yes, I got £ 15. 9. 5 from Curtis B. for *Dogskin*. They wrote that
a detailed report was following immediately, but it hasn't. Would you
ring them up? As I don't know what this money is for—American sales,
English sales, or English performing rights? It can hardly, however, be
for the latter, as I got the cheque on the 11th, when *Dogskin* had run
only a week and a half.[19]


                          Will write again soon.
                          Best love,
                          C.

February 23
Villa Alecrim do Norte
Sao Pedro
Sintra.

My darling Mummy,

    Here are some tiresome tasks, I'm afraid:

1. Enclosed cheque for £ 20.
2. Please pay with it my income tax (form enclosed) my year's subscription to *The Week* and keep change for your own expenses (not
   nearly covered by this, I know.)
3. Could you ring up William Jackson . . . and tell him—I thought I
   had—that "The Jack* and the Ell" was the *proposed* American title
   for *Mr Norris*. It appeared in the *catalogue* under that name. Later,
   as you know, I had it changed.

       *"Luck" is merely a misprint, I suppose.[20]
4. Would you pay this cheque for Barcley's (Curtis Brown) into my
   bank? It is for the first week and a half of *Dogskin*'s run (minus
   income-tax, etc).

                  Best love,
                  C.

March 1
Villa Alecrim do Norte
Sao Pedro
Sintra.


My darling Mummy,

Thank you very much for both your letters and for executing the various commissions. You are certainly worth ten agents put together: I'm sure that if you set up in business any author would prefer you to Curtis Brown; not that that is much of a compliment! That idiot Spencer C. B. is wrong, of course. Would you kindly ring him up again and once more ask him what the £ 15. 9. 5d were for? They were *not* performances, as I have since received £ 7. 11. 0 and £ 4. 16. 1d, for performances up to Feb 15th; very much less than C. B. promised. There was also £ 1. 6. 4 for the performances by the club in Nottingham. What I want to know is: are the £ 15. 9. 5d for English or American royalties, or both.

I have just got an advance copy of Forster's new book *Abinger Harvest* to review. it looks fascinating. I am to do a long signed review for the *Listener*. Two other reviews pending by me are Sean O'Casey's *Five Irish Plays* and of two books together: *Naval Odyssey* and *The Unambitious Journey*. A very poor effort by all concerned.

Wystan is said to be coming about the ninth. Could you get in touch with him and ask him to bring:
1. A copy of *Dogskin* (unless there is one in the drawer of the sitting-room bureau)
2. Any photographs he has of the production.

So glad you liked the lino-cut. The weather here stays bad. Our hens are dying at a great rate, nearly one a day. H. has his identity card all right. As for the bigger problem of the conscription, we shall have to deal with that in due course. It is no use worrying too much. The powers of hell are in the ascendant, these days, and one can only wait for better times and meanwhile learn something useful, like hen-farming. I think the life we are leading at present is far more satisfactory than anything we have tried before. The great thing is to be involved in one's surroundings and we are involved already, if only as English colonists. The word has gone round that we are such nice boys: and nice boys are a rarity in this colony of ladies. Three of them would be coming up to help us weed our garden this afternoon, if it weren't, thank Goodness, pelting with rain: so we shall go instead to hear Edward the Eighth say his over the wireless at the Mitchells. I told Miss Mitchell you were pleased with the lino-cut and she was delighted. *Paul is Alone* (not "Paul All Alone"!) progresses quite nicely. I was much amused by Muriel's letter, so were the others. "Our brave unhappy fleet" is really exquisite: A wonderful idea for a cartoon. Very sorry Mrs Dobson is so ill. Give R. my love when you write and express suitable sympathy if she dies. I will write to Henry."[71]

Best love,

C.

*[Handwritten notes on bottom of the page, not in Isherwood's handwriting:]*
March 7
Feb. 7 sent £15.19.5—Royalties on book from Faber & Faber (English not for American edition)
Feb 18 £7.11.0—fee on play for week ending Feb 8 & the 4 performances before Feb 1
Feb 21 £1.6.4 Four amateur performances at Nottingham

Feb 24 £4.16.1 fees on play for week ending Feb 15
March 3 £4.9.6 fees on play for week ending Feb 22

> yours faithfully,
> I O'Hea
> Dramatic Department

March 10
Villa Alecrim do Norte
Sao Pedro
Sintra.

My darling Mummy,

Thanks you so much for sending the copy of *Dogskin*. Where
did you get it from? I only wanted it to revise the text with, and if it
belongs to you I can send it back later.

Aren't things looking alarming in Europe? But I still have hopes
that it may all blow over and even turn out to have been the beginning
of a change. As long as nobody loses their heads; that's the real danger.
Hitler thinks he's being awfully clever, but I'm not sure.

If Wystan hasn't left by the time you get this, could you ask him
to bring out with him a small bottle of Pacita. It is the stuff for rabbits
and chickens and you can only get it at the Army and Navy stores. Also
a bottle of oil (anything they recommend) for curing dogs of worms?

Enclosed is a letter from Leonard Woolf. Clearly, it's no good
going on hedging with him: would you please ring up Curtis Brown

and tell them I definitely wish them now to explain the whole situation to him? I am also writing a note to Woolf myself.

Will write properly again in a day or two.

Best love,
C.


April 6
Villa Alecrim

My darling Mummy,

Thank you for your card and please forgive me; I have been so very busy that I haven't had a moment for writing. The play is now ready in rough draft and half of it, the first of the two acts, is typed out ready for the publisher. It is interesting, I think: far more so than *Dogskin* and far more experimental, as it is an attempt to blend absolutely straight acting dialogue, rather reminiscent of *Journey's End*, with various kinds of verse dialogue. The theme is really the life of Colonel Lawrence, but set into a climbing expedition on a big tropical mountain. It will be called: *The Ascent of F.6.* Wystan will stay here about a fortnight more, by which time I hope to have the whole thing ready for him to take back. We are also going to do a school composition book together; something quite new of its kind.[22] I also have seven books waiting to be reviewed! There is a great deal of minor news about local characters, but it will keep. So sorry your arm is bad. Yes, we have taken this house on for a year. Rather madly, considering H. is now liable at any moment to be plunged into difficulties with his passport, and conscription, but one lives from week to week. The weather is turning fine at last, the hens are doing well and the baby rabbit thrives. When are you coming out here? It would be fun if you could. Nothing from the Hogarth Press. Forster is said to have got through his operation nicely. I have written to him, but no answer yet. He may visit us later. Glad you like the review. I felt rather disgusted with it. Very difficult to do one's friends. Stephen writes en route for Greece. Henry has sent the money. In a week or two, we hope to begin to bathe.

I will write again soon.


Best love,
C.


Thank R. for his wonderful letters. Love to N.




April 13
Villa Alecrim do Norte
Sao Pedro
Sintra.


My darling Mummy,

Thank you very much for your Easter card. H. was also very pleased with his. By the time you get this, you will have heard from me, of course. This letter is just an unwelcome annex, in which I am going to be more than usually tiresome. Here is an income-tax form they sent me a day or two ago. As usual, it seems to have places for everything except the kind of income I get or earn. I am explaining my difficulties on a separate sheet. Would you be so kind as to go across to my bank and get them to pencil in the correct answers?

Last year, as you see, I just about doubled my income by writing.

Not a very wonderful achievement, but still, satisfactory. I hope that the excess tax paid on what passes through Curtis Brown's hands will just about balance whatever I should otherwise have to pay on earned income from the *Listener*. Or maybe I shall even get some back?

Well, the play is quite finished, corrections and all. Wystan will be bringing it back with him to England. He will see you, I hope, on his way through London. It all depends on the boat he catches. Now I have a big arrears of reviewing to make up. I have ten books waiting to be done! I hope *New Writing*, with my story in it, will be appearing soon.

The weather seems definitely on the up grade. On Good Friday we bathed, and it was lovely. There are glorious beaches here, quite deserted, all along the coast. One of the hens is broody and eggs are to be procured for her today No more news for the present. Will write again soon.

Best love,
C.

April 16
Villa Alecrim do Norte
Sao Pedro
Sintra.

My darling Mummy,

This is just to tell you that Wystan is leaving here in a few days, probably on Sunday. He will be arriving in London some time towards the end of next week and wonders if you could very kindly put him up for the night? I imagine you will; as you will then be able to hear a great deal of our news at first hand. In any case, Wystan will ring you up as soon as he gets to London, to hear whether it will be convenient for you to have him or not. There is not time for you to answer now, by letter.

Would you very kindly pay this cheque into my account? I have discovered that it is possible to sell review books and make a few shillings, despite the huge cost of postage.

Will write again properly soon.
Best love,
C.

April 23
Villa Alecrim do Norte
Sao Pedro
Sintra.

My darling Mummy,

Thank you for both your letters and so much for seeing about that ghastly income-tax. I now seem to have every variety of earned and unearned income. I have filled in the form and am sending it back today.

Not much news. The weather has been ghastly, but today is brighter. However, there are no real signs of a change yet, and we are almost on to another moon! I have been very busy and so has Heinz. He has made a big house for the chickens which we hope will hatch out in about a fortnight's time: I have started a serious effort to learn Portuguese, also I have been doing reviews—most of them rather spiteful, as I have a poisoned toe (it is better now)! At present, the *Listener* is due to publish: *Naval Odyssey, England Have My Bones, Seven League*

*Boots, Things Ancient and Modern,* and signed review of *Sir James Sexton, Agitator.* Also, yesterday, I restarted my novel.

It would be very nice indeed if you could come in June. I suppose there's no chance of getting Richard to join you? Nothing could be more English than this house. And the view, from this window, is very like the Yorkshire moors: so he ought to feel at home!

The only possible reason for postponing your visit might be that Forster would want to come out here for a few weeks when he is convalescent. I have invited him already, but haven't heard anything yet. However, I expect he's more likely to come later.

Could you please sent me some more 2d stamps for cheques?

What has happened about the things you bought for the dog? It there anybody who could bring them out?

Best love,
C.

May 24
Alecrim

My darling Mummy,

Thank you for your post-card and for attending to the driving-license. I am sorry you had to part with your photos. Here is another, which, if it isn't flattering, is at least historic: we had just finished *F6*! I hear, by the way that Doone wants some alterations. Wystan is going to see him about it on Saturday. I am rather impatient with Doone, and inclined not to agree. But we shall hear what they are.

Enclosed is another horrid little ploy, for when you get back from the north. The letter explains itself. In making my returns for 1934/35,

I didn't enclose this tax-deduction certificate: so here it is. It's the only one I have for that year. Maybe I shall get it back. It will nicely cover some of your numerous expenses for me lately.

As regards my British driving-license. Yes, I had one; but that was in the days before there was a test. You just bought it at an office. One of them, at least—they were only for one year each—should be in the same drawer of the bureau, if I've kept it at all. But anyhow I think my name is sure to be on some list or other. I believe that last license was for the year 1929. I got it to drive Mrs Lanigan's car in Scotland.[23]

Have just heard from Morgan.[24] There is certainly no immediate chance of his coming. He is still full of ailments, poor thing: and a creature called MacDonald is suing him for libel, on the article "A Flood in the Office" in *Abinger Harvest*.[25] He thinks he will certainly have to pay £ 500. Our libel law is too revoltingly idiotic for words. It simply gives an opportunity to these people who are nothing better than blackmailers.

I also heard from Robson-Scott, who would like to come early in July. So if you *could* come by the earlier of the two boats it would be better. But I shall write and ask him, of course, to come later in July, if he can manage it.

As for Ava, I'm hoping to find an excuse for not seeing her again.[26] She is not my sort. I have no use for people with brilliant hypnotic eyes and gestures like Ibsen characters. They simultaneously frighten and bore me; I prefer to be bored without being frightened, as we shall be this afternoon when we go to call on a very nice Portuguese advocate named Dr Olavo. Besides at Dr Olavo's house there are drinks, and very nice cake. He is determined to translate *Mr Norris,* which he hasn't yet read. *Mr Norris* has found its way into the English club at Lisbon, and Mrs Mitchell's daughter-in-law has read it![27] The word is going round that I am deeper than I look, and I am sure people are deciding that H. is a German spy. What a profession being a writer is!

The white rabbit has now had its litter, apparently. They are covered up in straw and we can't see them yet. The Mitchells have borrowed our buck. H. is building a skyscraper for the rabbits to live in. The sixteen chicks are all doing well.

Give my love to R. and Nanny and everybody up north, including specially all Monkhouses. I am contributing another section of *The Lost* to the next number of *New Writing*. It is about Frl Schroeder.[28] I think you have seen it. When *Paul* is finished, I shall definitely do a book of psuedo-memoirs, including "The Nowaks" "Evening at the Bay" more Berlin stuff, a sketch about life as a medical student and my Greek island diary.[29] E. S. P. Haynes is calling at Lisbon for one day next month on a cruise. "The Nowaks" has made a great hit with all my friends. Several people like it better than anything I've written. I am sorry, rather; because it's not the way I want to write. There is a fatal slickness about using the first person singular: you get bold coarse effects, but it's all very fake really, and arch and naughty—at any rate when I do it.

> Best love and best greetings
> from Heinz.
> C.

June 7
Villa Alecrim do Norte
Sao Pedro
Sintra.

My darling Mummy,

Thank you very much for your post-card. Yes, the driving permit arrived quite satisfactorily. I am amazed at the lack of formality. Thank you very much for getting it.

Since writing you last, I decided not to continue on the novel at present.[30] I hadn't been feeling comfortable about it for some time. The idea still interests me very much; but the construction must be quite different. It was far too loose and woolly. All my books seem to begin like that.

So I wrote immediately to Methuen and to Curtis Brown. To Methuen I proposed doing a book of autobiographical sketches, containing all the material of *The Lost* (including "The Nowaks") with four or five other pieces: "Evening at the Bay" (enlarged), a story about tutoring, a story about the medical school, my Greek diary and possibly a story about film work. To Curtis Brown I wrote that they were to get the best terms for me they could, try and arrange for me to keep the £ 150 advance, and, failing that, politely threaten a complete break-off of all dealings with Methuen for the future. I'm afraid they're not likely to handle this properly. It would be easy enough if I were there personally. However, for good or ill, I mean to write this book. Indeed, a good half of it is written already. I have all the manuscript of the old *Lost* with me here. Also my Greek diary. Also the necessary material for the film story. But there are still some papers in London I can't do without: would you be so kind as to bring them with you when you come?

1. The volume of *New Country*. I think my copy is in a drawer of the bureau.

2. The middle of the three diaries in your brown paper parcel. This terrible volume can be identified without the least contamination by simply noticing that its side-covers are much thicker than the other two! Or, if this is not immediately apparent, a glance at the top left hand corner of the first page will reveal the date it was started on, which must either 1925 or 1926!

3. In my playbox or in the bureau or in the chest of drawers, a big envelope full of papers. I don't know what is written on the outside. But I believe there are only two such envelopes in any case, and one of them

is "The Winter Term". I want the other. If there are three such envelopes, and two of them full of miscellaneous papers, please bring them
both, as you would hardly be able to find the funny little scrap I want.
It is about the medical school.

4. Possibly in one of these envelopes or loose in my playbox, an
orange exercise book belonging to Ian Scott-Kilvert, full of English
compositions, which I stole, while at the Langs, in preparation for *The
Day*.[31] But this, if you can't find it, is not terribly important.

5. My medical school exercise books. These, if not destroyed, are
in the little bookshelf beside the piano. I want them chiefly for local
colour. If they have disappeared, it doesn't frightfully matter. Robert
Moody will no doubt send me his.[32]

I hope these things won't be an awful nuisance in your suitcase.
But they shouldn't take up too much room, really. And anyhow the
journey will be more or less door-to-door. I shall, of course, meet you
on the boat.

The weather is heavenly. Brilliant sunshine. But up here it is
always nice and fresh. The five rabbits are all out of the nest now. The
other day, H. went to the casino and won seven hundred escudos, which
paid our coal bill and left enough over for twelve more hens! I hope
that the ducklings will hatch out during your visit. The chickens are
getting quite big now.

Henry wrote the other day rather alarmingly suggesting a tour of
Portugal, at which, I gather I should be expected to assist, in August!
Needless to say, he must be dissuaded from this idea, and indeed it could
be explained to him, with perfect truth, that Portugal is on the whole a
very uncomfortable place, with few good hotels! However, you will be
able to do that with authority after you've been here!

I have just heard from John Lehmann, who will be sending or
bringing you a bit of manuscript which I had sent him for the next
number of *New Writing* and which I had to ask him not to publish,

as if it is to be included in my new book it shouldn't previously appear. Will you bring this out with you too, please? It is quite short. Only twenty pages.

No more news for the present. Haynes is coming the day after tomorrow. Miss Mitchell has left for England. Mrs Mitchell is still here, but will doubtless have retired to stay with some people on the other side of the Tagus, before you come. Also Lady Carrick will have gone away. This is a pity, as she's quite nice, and you could have talked about Repton. Her rather unpleasant but attractive son, Ikerrin, was with me at the Hall. He left under a cloud, but she apparently doesn't know this, or doesn't know that I know!

Your arrival has created some talk in the colony. People are anxious to see you and make up their minds if I'm really respectable or not. *Mr Norris,* which somebody cattily contributed to the library of the ladies' club, has aroused certain doubts!

No more news from Robson-Scott. But I imagine all that will pan out satisfactorily.

Have just finished reading Dr Cronin's *The Stars Look Down*.[33] I think it is really one of the very best things of its kind that I have ever read. Of course, it's not great literature, but it's so well put together, so human, so honest, so interesting. Probably you read it ages ago. I don't recommend it, because it's very depressing, and you would agree, anyhow, with its politics, which are liberal-socialist. But every fascist, like Marjorie Ross, should be made to read it, because it's so quietly and unanswerably convincing.[34]

Must stop now. Best love,
C.

June 21
Villa Alecrim do Norte

My darling Mummy,

Thank you for your letter, which has just arrived. I am sorry
you're not arriving sooner, but if the boat is comfortable, that's the main
thing. I re-enclose the list. As you see, I really want very little. But do
try and find that scrap about the medical school if you can. Also an account of my visit to Basil Fry at Bremen, which I'm pretty sure is there,
in loose sheets, handwritten, very small.[35] It starts with our running to
catch the tramp steamer at the docks, and some rather indecent conversation with the captain. That's really all.

If you have time, could you bring with you two tubes of Gibbs'
S.R. toothpaste, which is good for stopping gum bleeding?

If you are absolutely forced to land, in order to go through the
customs with the other passengers, and if, by any chance, I'm not allowed on board, you can be certain that I shall be waiting at the dock-
gates. I assume that the boat will arrive in very early. They generally do.
I shall find this out, of course, at my end. And I shall be at the dock
round about 9. a.m. at the latest. You can rely absolutely on this. But
try not to land till after 9.

Have a nice trip. Take Mothersill, if you must, last thing at night
and first thing in the morning; otherwise not. But I advise only taking
it when you start, and then, if the weather is good, as it's almost sure
to be, leaving it off altogether and sitting as much as possible on deck.
Take perhaps one more at the *end* of the Bay of Biscay, which is much
rougher than the beginning, even in bad weather. But now I expect it
will all be like a millpond.

No point in sending any more news. All when we meet. I suggest you bring your sketching-block.

Best love,
Christopher

July 16
Sintra

My darling Mummy,

I intended writing to you yesterday, following my 'business' letter, but somehow the day went past without my finding time. So far, for better or worse, there is no news, either from Bruxelles or from the consulate here. Of course, I knew that Gerald couldn't arrange anything for a day or two now, so it's not surprising.

On Saturday evening, Robson-Scott and his friend duly arrived and on Sunday we all went over to Cascaes, where there was a regatta.[36] H. although we didn't know it, was also an onlooker, from the Mitchells' boat. His weekend seems to have been a success and he is now with Mrs Loweth, cutting down trees in the garden and learning tennis.[37] I only hope she'll be disposed to keep him for a bit longer yet. It is much the best place for him just now and he seems very happy. We bathed with him on Monday and I visited him on Tuesday.[38]

While at Cascaes, we ran into James Stern, who is a friend of Robson-Scott's, and has written an (apparently) good book of stories about South Africa called *The Heartless Land*. His wife is a German girl (the same whom I decided, on quite insufficient evidence, to be Frau Sternheim).[39] We know a lot of the same people, both in Berlin and London, and have a great deal in common.[40] I think they are coming to share this villa, as soon as Robson-Scott leaves, which will be a first step towards economy. She seems very practical and is quite prepared to take a go at the house-management. Also, as both her brothers are refugees, she is extremely able to sympathize with our difficulties. Stern himself is Irish and rather an invalid. He is none the better for his experiences in Rhodesia, which included being bitten by a rattlesnake.

Yesterday, I received a cheque from the Income-Tax people for £ 30. 10. 9d, which is all to the good. I don't quite know for which year this is; but I suppose for this last; it is roughly what they deducted on my Methuen advance. No money from Henry for the last quarter, yet.

Robson-Scott and his friend have been seeing the sights, while I stayed at home and tried, not very successfully, to restart work. I have done a little, however, on one of the Freshwater sketches.

I enjoyed your visit so much and did appreciate all your kindness and understanding of the situation.

Best love,
C.



August 28
83. rue Euphrosine Beerneart
Ostende

My darling Mummy,

I am writing this just after my telephone talk with you. I was very sorry to harass you like that, just after breakfast, but it is really necessary to be able to show the money now, as things are in train. Belgium is being prepared for immediate putting-through, should the other possibilities fail, but I am still anxious to see what Ecuador offers, and now Salinger has developed interesting connections with Mexico.[41] The latter would be completely above-board.

Anyhow, here is the signed slip; so please make arrangements now so that I can cash the cheque if necessary. You may rely on me to look after the whole business, as I am on the spot. But quick decisions may always become necessary and it is essential to be in a position to bargain.

We left the other pension after one meal as I didn't like it. Here it is very nice and I have two rooms, a little one to work in. Forster leaves tomorrow. He has enjoyed himself I think. H. is very well. The weather is heavenly. We are all just off to bathe.

My birthday was very nice. I wish you could have been there.

> Will write again soon.
> Best love,
> C.

September 3
[Ostende]

My darling Mummy,

Well, the money has duly arrived, as I told you in a post-card yesterday and as I told Robert to tell you on the telephone as soon as he arrived in England.[42] I saw Salinger yesterday, and have written to the Bank in Bruxelles telling them to transfer 700 into his account: he has an account at the same bank. I only hope that the people in London haven't made a muddle of this, as I feared they would; because I got this morning a letter asking me to sign a paper taking all responsibility for the depreciation of the money due to crises in the foreign exchange market. However, I am writing to Bruxelles saying what in hell do you mean by foreign exchange, my money is in English pounds, I hope? If it isn't, we must resign ourselves to losing anything up to fifty pounds on selling and reselling Belgian francs, as I pointed out to you on the telephone. However, it may be just a matter of form. I shall sign nothing till I hear definitely, of course.

Meanwhile we are hot on the track of Mexico. Salinger has very good connections with the Mexican officials here and thinks the whole thing could be arranged with them; absolutely legal, foolproof and above-board, without even leaving this country. So we've told him to make quite certain of this and let us know. Belgium is being brought to a point where all would be in readiness to take the final steps, but I have a deep rooted prejudice against Belgium if anything better can be found, and I know you have, too. Mexico might take two and a half months to put through, but we should know pretty soon definitely one way or the other. It would cost about the same. I think Mexico is more respectable if it can be managed, and it is a great advantage having people actually here in Bruxelles to deal with. The Ecuadorians are in Paris.[43]

Any news of the Burfords and my papers?[44] I had a letter from Jimmy Stern saying that he was packing them all up and that the Burfords would certainly take them. So that's that.

Not a word from Miss Mitchell.

We think of leaving for Bruxelles early next week. The weather here is going off, it seems, though very stuffy. I've bathed every day, so far. But we are both bored and miss our country life and regular occupations.

The latest mad idea: to got to Stockholm and learn massage there.

Best love,
C.

September 6
Ostende

Thank you for your card. Everything is all right afterall, about the money and I have Salinger's receipt. "Foreign currency" meant English money. Could you sometime soon post me the earlier volume of the two diaries which you still have in that parcel in your room? Better send it to Gerald's address—70 Square Marie Louise, Bruxelles, as we're certainly going there in a day or two, and mark "to await arrival". Could you begin negotiations with Miss Bradley for the recovery of my suitcases from Sintra? She might know of somebody to bring them? I would gladly pay 10/- per suitcase to cover tips, etc, on route. Of course, none of them are locked, but we must risk that!

Best love,
C.

September 11
23 Avenue Michel Ange
Bruxelles

Thank you for your card of yesterday and for card, letter and enclosures today. Please send the thing direct to this address—also the *1000 Words Spanish* and *Once your Enemy,* which I must review. Could you also find my little light green diary of the tour with G. B. Smith in the Alps and also *one* (never mind which) of my G. B. Smith history notebooks—if they still exist?[45] I want to write something about him and must recapture his "tone of voice". I will attend to the Stern's questions per telegraph from here. Not a word from *Miss* Mitchell. Very annoying.

All well. Preliminary conversation most encouraging. Next week a very big bug arrives and we hope to get things put through, quickly.

Best love,
C.

October 24
70 Square Marie Louise
Bruxelles

My darling Mummy,

I'm afraid it's ages since I last wrote. As you see, we're returned from Spa[in]. The weather was too awful. But the air did us both good. I'd been a little fluy myself, but that is all over now. And I returned with quite a promising start to my new book written. It really looks as if I might get on with it now. Then, we rapidly changed pensions, the first being a failure and are now in an apparently nice one, though I won't speak too soon. It is Pension La Source. 99 Rue de la Source. I give Gerald's address as being really safer, in case we may make another move. But all the addresses trickle through to me sooner or later.

Heinz is supposed to have another operation (on his nose) in about a fortnight. This time, poor thing, he's scared; but I supposed it will have to be done.[46] Meanwhile, Mexico had proceeded by leaps and bounds. As luck would have it, the *chargé d'affaires* at the Legation here has been appointed to a job in Mexico itself. And he has gone off taking with him copies of all the necessary documents about Heinz and

700 pounds, for which a receipt has been given. The deed will be done before the end of November, at the Consulate at Antwerp. Salinger now guarantees that the total amount, plus his expenses, will be under the thousand. He expects to return a little of it, that is to say, to us. I really and honestly think everything is as O-K as possible; always supposing something like a revolution doesn't break out in Mexico during the course of the next three weeks; and even then Salinger, who has lots of other interests in Mexico, thinks he can put things through. But we won't hilloo till we're out the wood: and not very loud, then.

In the meanwhile, we are taking steps to get an actual letter from the Legation here, acknowledging the whole transaction officially and promising specific time-limits. This letter shall be forwarded to you when received. For the present, best say *nothing* to anybody.

Did you see my review of the Hauser book in the *Listener* book supp? Also Morgan on *F.6*?

Longing to hear what you think of Edward's Hilda: and what they chose as presents.[47]

The Sterns aren't going to Mexico for the present, though they still intend to do so in the spring.

Have just finished Stephen's new book. Very good, but not your [cup of] tea. Just politics.[48] I haven't forgotten that you're to have *The London Girl in the 80s,* but haven't reviewed it, yet.

No more news, I think.

Best love,
C.

October 31
99 rue de la Source
Bruxelles

Thank you very much indeed for your letter. Sorry R. isn't well. My sympathies to Henry. I will write to him very soon but have been so busy.

Yes this address is all right to send things to, now: we look like being here some time. The date of the new operation is still uncertain. Surrealism tries to express life in terms and images of the world of dreams. Brian Howard has a toasting-fork face because the artist thinks a toasting-fork face expresses his personality more truly and essentially than his own face. If you knew Brian well, I think you'd agree. I'm sorry Edward didn't take the Lichtenberg as well. Didn't he like it? Let me know what the framing costs. The great mistake people make about surrealism is to try to "understand" it. An odd dream doesn't need to be understood to be appreciated. Would you please ask the Bank how my account stands now?

Best love,
C.

November 8
99 Rue de la Source
Bruxelles

My darling Mummy,

Thank you for your card and for all the press cuttings. There is really no news. The book progresses, and the rain pours down, and the time steadily approaches when the *Daily Mail* will have to admit that in encouraging Franco it was betraying the British Empire to Mussolini. Against this incredible background of idiocy, my reminiscences of the twenties seem like the chatter of a nursery governess over the tea-table; but perhaps that's as well. It will prevent the book being pompous. Did you see that the Pope has ordered the middles of MichelAngelo frescoes in the Vatican painted over, where necessary, with drapery? How can anybody remain catholic? Tell Henry and Graham Greene.

This is a very nice pension.

Now news of the operation. We think the doctor must be involved in a Rexist plot. He seems to have no more interest in surgery at all.

First messages arrived from Mexico City. Our man is there and has begun the fell deed. A telegram awaited in five or six days, definitely confirming this: and then, finally, the necessary papers by air mail. Speaks perfect American.

The balance is an awful shock. It means that I have only thirty pounds actually saved. And the two hundred is down to one hundred and five! All these moves cost so much. And, to cap it all, I now hear that there is no cash coming in from U.S.A. for *Dogskin*. We've had it all already, they say. This is almost certainly a swindle, but what is one to do? Curtis B. didn't even draw up the contract, so they aren't really responsible. I can't help feeling that they're not on our side. I wish I could find an efficient honest agent.

I had a very nice letter from R. Please thank him.

Best love,
C.

November 22
99 Rue de la Source
Bruxelles

My darling Mummy,

It's a long time since I wrote, but also a long time since I heard from you! And I expect Robert[49] will have told you our news, such as it is. At last, thank Goodness, it has stopped raining and begun to freeze. I am very busy with my book. I hope to have a good half of it finished by Christmas and the whole thing by the end of January—with luck! Then there are the review books, not very thrilling, and far too many of them. Which reminds me, not a single word from Lisbon as to the fate of my books and our clothes. I'm afraid young Miss Mitchell, though so well-intentioned, has gone Irish and vague at the prospect of making a list of the books, as she promised, quite of her own accord, to do. I must write her again, I suppose.

Would you please look in my manuscript drawer and see if you can find a big envelope containing my so-called "Berlin Diary" (the 'written' one; not the genuine one, which you have in your room). The envelope ought to contain an original manuscript, stuck on to bits of stronger paper, and the beginnings of a copy. I want the whole thing; because John Lehmann wants to publish it in Number Three of *New Writing*; as there is absolutely no prospect of getting hold of Jean and obtaining her consent to the publication of "Sally Bowles."[50] *If* you happen to hear anything about her, do do your best. Time is getting short.

Since Robert left, we interviewed the doctor telephonically, and he seemed to think he'd operate this coming week. He'll let us know. These delays are really infuriating.

I've seen a lot of good films, mostly French: *Under Western Eyes, Mayerling, Jenny, Club de Femmes, These Three*. Also *Mutiny on the Bounty*.

*Rembrandt* is coming here very soon, now.

We continue to like this pension. The proprietress has just had an awful tragedy: her son, twenty-six years old, killed in a motor-accident. She has gone off to Paris, where it happened.

Some possibility of Stephen coming for Xmas.

No news of "F.6."

Best love,
Christopher

December 2
99 Rue de la Source

My darling Mummy,

Thank you for your letter.

I haven't answered it before because I've been so busy—making an effort to get a big chunk of my book finished before Xmas. At present, 2 chapters are ready, and I hope to have the third written by next Monday, at latest. That will cover the whole of Repton and Cambridge. After, that, there'll be four more chapters—one for each year, up to 1929.[51]

It's awfully interesting work. I think it might be the best thing I've done so far: but the dangers are that the whole thing may become too genial, or merely a series of archly risky revelations, or so private as to be quite incomprehensible. I have to make it very objective—and yet not sneer. The things which were important to me *then* have to be treated with a kind of respect: and yet quite calmly taken to pieces and examined. Another problem is how to cut down the number of characters by three quarters without unnecessarily distorting the facts. I want to build the whole book round a small group of people—G. B. Smith, Edward, Hector, the Quartet (if possible hardly mentioning Olive— though this seems difficult!) Lichtenberg, Wystan, Maunder, Moody.[52] I shall possibly call it "The North West Passage"—because a good deal of the book is taken up with explaining *why* I wanted to write a novel with that name, exactly *what* view of life is contained in that title, etc.

I write all this, and pick up the paper, to read that Hitler seems to be intervening quite openly in Spain. The prospects of one's getting literary work finished without interruption don't seem too brilliant—but I only ask to be given till the end of January!

Further plans (Hitler permitting) are still very uncertain. No more news from across the water. Heinz's idiot doctor *still* doesn't summon him to be operated: the clinic is full. If the call doesn't come soon, we must postpone it. I won't have him ill at Xmas.

The *Listener* hasn't printed any more of my reviews—so I'm not writing any new ones. November is the first month for years that I haven't earnt a penny!

Young Miss Mitchell writes that Mrs Norton has actually *come* to England, bringing my books![53] But where is she? Would your next-door neighbor know?

Not a word from Jean.

If you hear of anybody coming to Brussels, they might bring my skates!

Much as I should like to see you, I *can't* recommend Bruges. Even in summer, it is full of medieval darkness—and in winter it must be depressing beyond words. It is much more sinister than the Dutch towns.

No more news. Am *quite* well again. Have heard that my complaint was probably a kind of internal flu which is sweeping Brussels now.

What news of Edward?

What do you say to Stephen's marriage? (If you didn't know, I'm sure Olive will have all details).[54]

Best love—and to R. and Nanny.
Christopher

December 7
99 rue de la Source

No answer to my letter. Did you get it? Miss M. swears she sent list of books to London address and has dispatched most of the books themselves with Mrs Norton, weeks ago. No news? And Jean? Would you please ring up Cape and ask them if they know whether O'Brien has sent off the fees and complimentary copies of *Best Short Stories 1936* yet?[55] Because he *may* have sent mine to Portugal. I wrote him direct: no answer.

H. was operated today. He certainly looks a nasty mess at present, poor thing—just a mouth wide open groaning surrounded with bandages. But the doctor seems satisfied. I hope to find him a little better tomorrow.

Ghastly weather—rain and snow.

Best love,
C.

December 22
99 Rue de la Source
Brussels

My darling Mummy,

Thank you so much for your letter and cards and for the money.
Heinz will thank you, separately; but he does now, too. He is buying
a shirt with his. I think I shall get Wells' *The Croquet Player*. Have you
read it?

We look like having quite an assembly for Christmas. There will
be Tony and Humphrey Spender, and Robson-Scott and his friend Rico
Bixner; and Gerald, of course. And Wentworth. Wentworth is just a
young man who has taken a flat here. He writes. Not very thrilling, but
quite amiable and hospitable. He has cash. I plan to have our Christmas
party in his flat.

Heinz's nose is now quite restored; there is only the slightest scar,
which will disappear in a day or two. As soon as he's scarless, we'll have
a photo taken and I'll send you a copy. We had one done just before the
operation, to compare.

I am hoping to get a lot of news from Tony; notably about
Stephen and his bride. What on earth made him have such a stupid
wedding? For the moment, I'm even more excited by the suggestion
very vaguely made in Olive's letter (she's always so terrified of police-
spies) that Wystan is going to Spain. Can you ask about this? Because
I may be wrong. But if Wystan is going, I must urgently send a message to Edward to let me have *his* copy of a story called "The Railway
Accident", which I want to quote in my book.[56] I finished chapter four
about an hour ago, only one day behind schedule. I am quite fairly
pleased with it so far, though what any outside person would think of it
is a question. But anyhow, it's a good thing to get it all written down; a
sort of "M.S. found in a bottle" which might interest people later. The

handling of the Mangeot question is perhaps the greatest tour-de-force of tact achieved by this generation. André I've boosted to the skies.

There is no news from America yet, but this doesn't alarm me unduly. I know how long everything takes. Now, by great good luck, our lawyer, who has big interests in the country quite apart from our concern, is going over there early in January for a month and promises he won't return without having fixed everything; always supposing that there's no news earlier.

I wrote to Mrs Mitchell, enclosing a cheque for a pound and asking her to post the rest of the books to Pembroke Gardens. Any other method of transport seems so unreliable. I cannot imagine what Mrs Norton has done with the books she had. I hope she hasn't died in childbirth? I told Mrs M. in my letter that they'd never been delivered. It's annoying, because the first lot included my book of press-cuttings and a copy of *All the Conspirators,* which can't, now, be replaced.

Thank you for Muriel's funny letter. What a mix-up she's in. The Archbishop seems to have confused her still further. What does Marjorie Ross say? It is generally believed on the Continent that Edward was really kicked out because of the Nazi influence in his entourage: in that case, why can't the slimy old hypocrite have the courage to say so, instead of trying to make it a moral issue?[57]

Well, all the season's greetings to you and Richard and Nanny. Maybe I'll send some cards, but there's an awful rush of Christmas letters to write. I had to finish my chapter first.

Not a word from Jean.

C.

Best love and thank you so much
for your present. Heinz

*"Lady into Fox": a picture of Kathleen from Isherwood's childhood photo album.*

*Isherwood's passport photo, in which he sports a rather unfortunate haircut.*

*Isherwood in Berlin.*

*Isherwood and the artful Gerald Hamilton.*

*Gerald Hamilton in his eccentric glory.*

*Jean Ross, the "model"*
*for Sally Bowles.*

*Two photographs*
*from E. M. Forster's*
*visit to Isherwood*
*in Brussels.*
*Top: Isherwood,*
*Forster, and two*
*unidentified men.*
*Bottom: Forster,*
*Isherwood, an*
*unidentified man,*
*and Gerald Hamilton.*

*Klaus Mann.*

*Left: Roger and Stella Burford. Right: Isherwood and Roger Burford, who had been a friend at Cambridge.*

At Ostende 1936

Forster, Heinz, Moody

*Top: By the sea with Gerald Hamilton, E. M. Forster, Heinz, and Robert Moody, Ostend, 1936. Bottom: On the beach with an overdressed Forster, Heinz, and Moody, Ostend, 1936.*

*E. M. Forster was a welcome visitor throughout Isherwood's peripatetic thirties.*

*Heinz and Isherwood, always searching for a new nationality for Heinz.*

*Heinz. Isherwood wrote to Kathleen that Heinz loved animals.*

*Stephen Spender
and Tony Hyndman.*

*Inez Spender (née Pearn),
the wife of Stephen Spender.*

*Cuthbert Worsley, journalist and former lover of Tony Hyndman. Worsley and Spender went to Spain in 1936 on assignment for the* Daily Worker.

*A newly shorn Humphrey Spender in Portugal. Isherwood wrote that he shaved his hair to make it grow better and "refuses to be seen without a cap."*

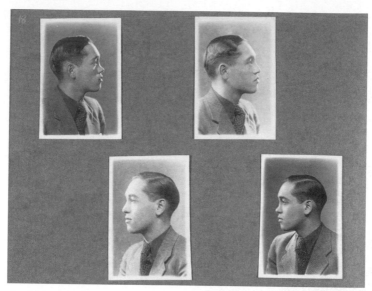

*Building a bridge: before and after shots of Heinz's new nose. Although Isherwood had always loved Heinz's smashed-in nose (the result of a childhood fight), it caused numerous breathing problems. Despite their residence and passport troubles, Isherwood made the surgery a priority.*

*Top: Giles Romilly, the rebellious nephew of Winston Churchill, whom Isherwood found "highly decorative." Bottom: Tony Hyndman. After Spender married Inez, Hyndman and Romilly became friends, and the two went together to fight in Spain.*

*Tony (Toni) Altmann,*
*Brian Howard's*
*troublesome boyfriend.*

*Tania Stern*
*at the villa in Portugal.*

*William Robson-Scott
was a good friend
to Isherwood during
the thirties, especially
during Heinz's trial.*

*Isherwood at work.*

*E. M. Forster,
Dover, 1937.*

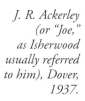

*J. R. Ackerley
(or "Joe,"
as Isherwood
usually referred
to him), Dover,
1937.*

*Jean (last name unknown) and W. H. Auden.*

*W. H. Auden, Dover, 1937.*

*Possibly Auden, in awkward repose.*

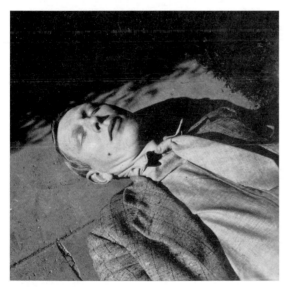

*Auden in a candid moment.*

*W. H. Auden. Isherwood felt that America had separated him from Auden.*

*Auden, Spender, and Isherwood. Spender claimed, "We were the 1930s."*

December 26
99 rue de la Source
Bruxelles

Thank you so much for the little diary. I was so glad to get it. I'll write to Jack, Kearsey and Rachel in due course.[58]

About that sherry—would you send it to Stephen, as a kind of wedding present? He has to do a lot of entertaining, so may appreciate it. His phone number is Riverside 3990. If he doesn't want it, keep it for guests.

Tony and Giles Romilly are here.[59] We've had a nice Xmas.

Best love,
C.

Hotel Gaisser.
Luxembourg.    May 5   1937

still here. Salzinger promises
news by the end of this week:
I hope he's right! Otherwise,
all goes well. We're having
nice weather, on the whole. I'll
write you all details when I
get to Brussels. The French
report turned out, of course, to
be wildly exaggerated. Gueld
visited us yesterday, but has
left again today.
            Best love.   C.
        Best greetings
            Heinz

Mrs Bradshaw. Isherwood

19 Pembroke Gardens

LONDON   W 8

Angleterre.

# 1937

This is an extremely traumatic year
for Isherwood. He is plagued by guilt
that his friends are all going to Spain, and he and Auden meet in Paris
as Auden heads off to do his bit in the Spanish civil war. Isherwood
doesn't do much new writing, but he attends the rehearsals in London
for *The Ascent of F6*, which premieres at the Mercury Theatre in February. Later in the year, he works with Auden in Dover on the play *On
the Frontier*, and he finishes *Lions and Shadows*. The Hogarth Press
published *Sally Bowles*, which would later be included in *Goodbye
to Berlin*.

On the domestic front, which in 1937 cannot be separated
from the political front, Hitler and world events finally catch up with
Isherwood and Heinz. Isherwood takes Heinz to Paris, where Heinz
gets into trouble with the police and is asked to leave the country. On
the advice of the shady lawyer, Salinger, he goes to Luxembourg to
wait for his Mexican passport, and Isherwood joins him there. When
Heinz is forced to leave Luxembourg, he goes to Trier with Salinger,
who promises to arrange for a new Belgian visa. Salinger insists that
Isherwood return to Brussels and wait for them, which he reluctantly
does. Heinz is granted a Belgian visa, but on the way back to the hotel
he is arrested by the Gestapo. Heinz's trial takes place in June. He is

found guilty and sentenced to six months in prison, a year of labor, and two years of military service.

Isherwood returns to London and works on a film for Alexander Korda. He spends most of the second half of the year in England, as he and Auden prepare to go abroad.

January 2
Rue de la Source
Brussels

My darling Mummy,

Thank you for your letter and cards. I enclose four photographs of Heinz, two before and two after the operation. Please show them to Olive and anybody else who is interested and then return them.

Henry writes today to say that he *may* pay some money into my bank account next week, provided he gets his from Marple. So I hope that, in accordance with my card, you put in enough to cover me: I drew a cheque for £ 20 today? As soon as he pays, I will send you a cheque for that amount.

Here is a review: at last. Please put it with my other cuttings in the envelope. I have just had an offer from a firm called Robert Hale to translate some lyrics taken from Brecht's *Dreigroschenoper* ("Three Groschen Opera") which is the great German classic of the twenties, and a kind of modernized and socialized version of *The Beggar's Opera*, with entirely different music and words.[1] I think it would be very interesting, but they only want to give me ten pounds. I am holding out for more, as it means quite a lot of work. Here are some verses from one of the songs I've already done. You'll notice that the name Macheath is taken from *The Beggar's Opera*; but the *Dreigroschenoper* is supposed to take place at the time of the Boer War.

> For the shark, he has his teeth and
> You can see them in his face;

And Macheath, he has his knife but
Hides it in a different place.

Down along the Thames green waters
Suddenly there's someone falls
Not from plague and not from cholera
It's Macheath has paid his calls.

And Schmul Meier still is missing,
Many a rich man's been removed
Mackie Messer has their money
But there's nothing can be proved.

Where is Alfons Glite, the cabman?
Will that ever see the day?
Some there are, perhaps, who know it—
Mackie Messer couldn't say.

Burnt alive were seven children
And an old man, in Soho—
Midst the crowd stands Mackie Messer,
Isn't asked and doesn't know.

For the shark has fins of crimson
When his victim's blood is shed,
Mackie Messer keeps his gloves on
And you cannot see the red.

I hope Wystan will come here on his way to the south. It is awful to think of his going.[2] Goodness knows where Tony is now.[3]

Forster comes on the 15th. Stephen on the 20th.
No news from Portugal?

Best love,
C.


January 18
99 Rue de la Source
Brussels

My darling Mummy,

A long time since I wrote and such a lot has happened.

On Monday a week ago, I finished the *Dreigroschenoper* translations. That afternoon a telegram arrived from London from Wystan,
who still hadn't left, saying he was crossing to Paris that night on route
for Spain and would I come to Paris on the Tuesday to meet him. So
of course I did. I found him with a very bad cold and a batch of letters
of introduction to the authorities in Valencia, where he hopes to get a
job with the ministry of propaganda. Failing this, he will work with the
Red Cross Unit or do auxiliary newspaper work, either at Valencia or
in Madrid. All that stuff in the papers is inaccurate and partly mali-
cious nonsense, as Wystan had particularly asked the journalists in
London not to print anything about him till he was actually in Spain,
for fear of getting him into trouble.[4] But anyhow, if he doesn't fight,
he breaks no law of ours. He is going entirely at his own expense and
quite alone, not with any unit. The *Daily Mail*, I suppose, would hint
that he was earning a pound a day! We spent Tuesday and Wednesday
together and I went off Wednesday evening, having seen the Sterns,

who have a lovely flat on the Notre Dame island, overlooking the Seine,[5] and Brian Howard, who was over visiting Tony Altmann, now permanently installed in Paris.[6] Wystan was very upset because all his luggage had been sent on in advance, by mistake, to the Franco-Spanish frontier, and he wasn't sure if he'd ever see it again. He promised faithfully to send me a wire before crossing into Spain, but he never has. This may mean anything. But probably only that there was too much of a rush.

Well, meanwhile, Salinger was doing his best to unearth Heinz's record at the Home Office.[7] The result was neither as bad or as good as we had expected. The official reason why H. was refused admissions is definitely 'moral'.[8] Salinger, who happened to be in London and saw the people personally, said, of course, what nonsense: Mr Neddermeyer was going to stay with Mrs Isherwood. Mr I. wouldn't even be present in England. And anyhow Mr Neddermeyer was the most respectable of persons, enjoying the friendship of such well-known Englishmen as Mr E. M. Forster, who would be prepared to vouch for him. (Morgan is actually writing a letter to this effect). Forster's name made a great impression on the Home Office people, Salinger said. Indeed, he came back from London convinced that the whole business would go off smoothly. But on Saturday, we heard that the application had been provisionally refused for the present. Unofficially, however, we have been advised to try again later in the year. The explanation is that the authorities are being very strict because of the coronation and not reversing any black marks, on principle, until that is over.[9] In any case, it is encouraging to know that H. is not regarded as in any way permanently stigmatized. Indeed, the officials admit that he was only excluded on suspicion in the first place and that they may quite well have been wrong. Salinger has been very energetic and really personally kind about all this and he isn't charging for the work he has done. I think he would appreciate it very much if you sent him a short note, thanking him for his trouble. Would that be too much of a nuisance?

As for Mexico. Not a word. But Salinger is definitely going there at the end of this month and should be able to stir them up. I am honestly not very alarmed about that business, knowing how casual Spaniards are. However, I go on exerting the maximum pressure at this end. If nothing is done before Salinger's arrival, we still ought to hear definitely by cable from him in Mexico City about three and a half weeks from now. His is a rush visit, and he'll go the quickest way, flying from New York.

Meanwhile, when I was in Paris, I had a serious talk with the Sterns about Heinz and his future as a masseur. And Tania said he could certainly get his tuition in Paris from a German exile masseur and she would give him tuition herself in the brand of physical culture she practises. So I've decided that, expensive as it may be, we will move to Paris as soon as possible. I'd like to live in Paris for a bit, anyhow. And, as soon as he was installed, I'd come to England for a fortnight or three weeks. Even getting to France isn't easy nowadays, but Salinger hopes to manage a visa for us in about ten days from now, which would mean that we'd leave Brussels at the end of this month, and I might come to London during the first week of February. How would that suit you?

How about Stephen, you ask? Well, I know nothing. Wystan was very alarmed and pessimistic about him.[10] A correspondent who knows Spain had said that, if he's really got behind the rebel lines and they discover who he is he may even be not merely expelled or imprisoned but shot. That I doubt, but an accident is always possible. I suppose Olive knows nothing? Or his wife?

Needless to say, my trip to Morocco is automatically off. Well, well, perhaps that's for the best. You know my inquisitive nature. Mr Norris leaves the day after tomorrow.

Forster and Buckingham came here Friday night and left again on Sunday afternoon. We enjoyed their visit: so did they, I think.

Robson-Scott has at last seen Heinz's uncle and aunt. They were very nice to him, said how could they ever thank you and me for keeping him out of Germany and implored him never to return under this regime. The grandmother is very bad but not dead yet, and I still hope she'll pull through the winter, as it will upset H. particularly if she died just now, when everything is rather depressing. The weather is enough to drive one to suicide. Endless mild days of rain. I long for the sun. I expect London is bad. Paris was.

My book has been at a standstill lately, owing to all these diversions. But now I am sitting down to it again, as there seems likely to be this delay with our Paris visa. I had been prepared to leave tomorrow or Wednesday, so was very jumpy and restless.

In Paris, a good film: *Sabotage*. Have you seen it?

Annoyed my press-cutting book is lost. Am sending a letter to Mrs Mitchell via Gerald. He could pick up the things when his boat calls on the return journey. It touches Lisbon both ways.

Tell Olive my news, but maybe don't mention Mr Norris' voyage. She'll only imagine some penny-dreadful intrigue.[11]

Best love,
C.


May 5
Hotel Gaisser
Luxembourg


Still here. Salinger promises news by the end of this week: I hope he's right! Otherwise, all goes well. We're having nice weather, on the whole. I'll write you all details when I get to Bruxelles. The French report turned out, of course, to be wildly exaggerated.[12] Gerald visited us yesterday, but has left again today.

Best love,
C.

Best greetings, Heinz.

[August 17]
9 East Cliff
Dover[13]

Thanks for forwarding letters. The first act is nearly ready.[14] Please remember the M.S. for Sylvain.[15] Weather good and both well. Never got the Macmillan letter.

Love,
C.

[August 30
Dover]

Thank you for your letter and sending money from Jack. Will you please send lots of flowers and fruit to Stephen—Hampstead Nursing Home, 40 Belsize Grove. N.W. 3? He's operated today. Spend *at least* 10/-. The play is as good as finished.

C.

Canton. March 3.
We're off tomorrow to Hankow, by
train — as our arrangements to go
by car have broken down. It is
very warm here: it will be much
colder, we hear, up north. The
Japanese air-raids here have been
far from alarming, since we came
and anyhow we're living outside
the town. Will write from Hankow
if possible. Both well. love
to all.                                    C.
Travelling is very bad for the figure. We
are both getting slimmer. Wystan

BY AIR VIA
IMPERIAL
AIRWAYS

POSTAGE

CORRESPONDENCE                    ADDRESS

2 Bradshaw. Isherwood
Pembroke Gardens
LONDON      W 8.

England

4.3.88/16
CANTON

VICTORIA
HONG KONG
7 MR 35 AM

# *1938*

Isherwood and Auden go to China to write *Journey to a War,* and most of the year is spent in activities relating to this book, although *Lions and Shadows* is published by the Hogarth Press in March. When the two are in China, German troops enter Austria, and Hitler declares the union of the two countries. On their way back from China, Auden and Isherwood stop in New York. Europe is speeding toward war as Hitler makes plans to annex the Sudetenland region of Czechoslovakia. In September, Chamberlain, Daladier, Hitler, and Mussolini meet in Munich to partition Czechoslovakia. Britain and France begin to mobilize, and Auden and Isherwood meet in Brussels to complete *Journey to a War.*

[Paris]
January 19
Wednesday night


Safely arrived so far, after a good journey. We had half a dozen photographers waiting for us at Victoria, and, judging from the numbers of pictures they took, the papers tomorrow will be full of nothing else. We leave for Marseilles tomorrow night.[1]

Christopher

[Marseilles]
January 21
Friday

Safely arrived here and have got our things on board. We're still uncertain whether or not to change to first class. Lovely weather. The boat sails at noon. Not many passengers, apparently.

Love to all,
Christopher

Colour [?]—much better. All well,
Wystan

[Cairo]
January 26
Tuesday

We are making a dash to Cairo, and rejoining the boat at Suez to-morrow. A nice voyage, though cool. The co. have given us *2* cabins—one to work in, gratis!

Next stop, Djibouti.
Christopher

The Egyptian police are supposed to be returning our passports to the boat, so we hope for the best. Having a nice time. Wystan

DJIBOUTI — Retour en brousse

[Djibouti]
January 29

Arrived here for a few hours this afternoon. It is absolutely lovely—everything the travel magazines tell you, but hotter, noisier, brighter, smellier, altogether more gorgeous. We are enjoying ourselves greatly—though the days at sea are dull.

Christopher

KANDY, LAKE FROM LADY HORTON'S WALK. CEYLON.

[Ceylon]
February 4

Arrived Colombo and got your letter—very many thanks. This is the loveliest country you can imagine—as though Kew Gardens had overgrown the whole of England. We have dashed up to Kandy by car to see the temple, and are leaving, alas, tonight. Singapore next. Best love, C.

On *no* account sign any contract for our new play with Rupert until you hear from me.[2]

Both well and getting quite brown  Wystan

February 8
[aboard ship]

My darling Mummy,

I am writing this on the eve of our arrival at Singapore and will
air-mail it to you from there—after I've seen if there's by any chance
another letter from you waiting for me.

What is there to say about this voyage? That, so far, it has been
very pleasant—if also intensely boring. The sea, as I write, is no bluer
than it might easily be off Brighton. The sun is hot, certainly, but you
can lie in it without the smallest ill effects, provided you cover your
head. Our cabin is as cool as could be expected. All the people on the
boat are dullish, except for a rubber-king, and a Hungarian photographer who has been in Spain and is going out to get war pictures on the
Chinese front. Our stops—in Egypt, at Djibouti and in Ceylon—were
all fascinating; I only wish they had been longer. It is true, in a way, to
say that the places look like their photographs, but they don't feel
like them—and what is so impossible to describe is the shock of actually meeting an elephant, or an arab with a camel, or even one of the
tropical trees from the Kew conservatory, in its native surroundings.
As for saying that all places are alike—Djibouti is more like Colombo
than Regent's Street is like Church Lane, Marple. There is a great deal
of vulgarity and ugly Westernisation in Colombo, of course; but then
the people are so amazing: no words can describe their beauty. We have
already written a great deal of material for the book. The voyage out
will form a whole section to itself.

If Rupert wants you to sign a contract for *On the Frontier*—the
important thing is to see that there's no clause giving him or the Group
Theatre any share whatever of the film rights. He may have his share
of the broadcasting and television, however. And, of course, no share

whatever in the book rights. He agreed to all this while I was in England, but there's no knowing what he'll do behind our backs.

*Singapore.* Very early.

This place might easily be Liverpool. Terrific but agreeable heat. Nothing from you, so will write again from Hong Kong.

Love, also to Richard and Nanny,
Christopher


February 19
Saturday
Hongkong Hotel
Hong Kong


My darling Mummy,

We got here last Wednesday, to find your two letters, for which many thanks. The photos were certainly amusing: you don't say if the typescript of those parts of *The Lost* has been duly sent from the metropolitan typewriting bureau, or not? But probably they weren't ready when you wrote. The hardest thing to remember here is that there is this enormous time-lag. Except for you, I haven't heard a word from anybody. Nothing from Stephen, nothing from Curtis Brown, nothing from little Chisholm, who'd promised me that address.[3] Nothing from Heinz. Nothing from Ian.[4] I am really alarmed about Ian, because he particularly told me that he was writing air-mail. I sent him a cheap rate cable two days ago—no answer. I wonder if you could find out if he's all right? Caius—if the number isn't in the written book you have to ask for *Gonville* and Caius. Maybe he's got my address wrong. And the messagerie offices here don't seem too efficient.

Hongkong is like Birmingham—a horrible town of banks guarded by cruisers, in one of the loveliest harbours in the world. We are living in a bathing cabin—very luxurious—out at Repulse Bay. We stay here about ten days: then to Canton, Hankow and Chungking. Don't be alarmed if you read about air raids—all reports are wildly exaggerated; and there are no Jap troops down here—only a few warships.

We move in very high circles. Yesterday we met the Ambassador, who adores "Sally Bowles" and will help us a lot in the interior. We may even travel with him. The military governor . . . we'll see in a day or two—also the Bishop. And we've met all the University professors. Everybody very helpful and hospitable. In a few days we'll go to stay with one of them. Tonight we dine with Bartlett, of the *News Chronicle*. Do you remember Baines, my contemporary at Repton? He's here, too. Peter Fleming is expected.[5]

The weather is cool and cloudy, but agreeable. You'd never think we were in the tropics.

Wystan sends his love—and would you please ring up his mother and give her this news?

Love to all,
Christopher

February 22
Hongkong
[cable]

Worried because Ian has never written can you find out if ill and cable me both send love = Christopher

February 25
c/o D. J. Sloss, Esq.
The University
Hongkong

My darling Mummy,

Please note the above address. Mr Sloss is the Vice-Chancellor of the University. He is putting us up all this week, and has been extraordinarily kind. He says that he'll act as poste restante for our letters in future. So always write to him.

Having letters sent to the messageries was really a great mistake. The staff is almost entirely Chinese, very vague about names and address, and 3 Icehouse Street is a huge building, of five stories. Hence all this fuss about Ian's, and, I suspect, other letters. Because I'd told plenty of people that 3 Icehouse St. was sufficient. So when, on the day of our arrival, I cabled Ian, and he cabled back, I never got the cable: hence my anxiety. However, this cable has now turned up, because when I cabled *you*, I gave my address here, and they immediately sent Ian's cable on from the office: it had been returned to them there. I presume Ian explained this to you when you rang him up, and that's why you didn't answer my cable to you? It only goes to show how dangerous it always is to give addresses in advance.

Our plans are now fairly definite. Having thoroughly sampled English colonial life (last night we dined with the Governor!) we leave on Saturday afternoon for Macao, the Portuguese colony on the mainland. Back here on Sunday. Then off on Monday to Canton, by riverboat, which is perfectly safe. There we stay three days. Then by car to Hankow. Then up the Yangtze to Chungking. Then back to Hankow, and return to Hongkong. This will be our first and most important journey. It may take a month, or even two. The posts are so disorganized that it will probably be impossible to write, though I certainly will if I can do; but don't be in the very least alarmed if you hear nothing. If I haven't written, I'll cable you when we arrive back here.

There's no other news, I think. The weather is still cool, but bright and sunny. The view from my windows is marvellous. We are both keeping very well. I have been vaccinated, as the Chinese authorities seem to like it. It hasn't taken at all. The Colony is still full of rumours of the approach of Peter Fleming; some even say that he is here, incog. The atmosphere here is so enormously peaceful and English that it is hard to realize that there's a war anywhere within a thousand miles. The size of China seems to swallow everything. Even now, it will still be possible to make an enormous journey, as we are doing, without going anywhere near the trenches.

Will you please communicate with Curtis Brown about whether *Lions and Shadows* has or hadn't been accepted in America? I've never heard a word. As regards "Sally Bowles" in *Harper's Bazaar,* I agree with whatever you say, of course. I doubt, though, if you'll get a hundred. Incidentally, the money earnt in America is not liable to tax, provided that I am out of England during six months of the tax year. I think that's right?

Best love, and to R. and Nanny. I hope the house-cleaning goes off well.

C.

March 3
Canton

We're off tomorrow to Hankow, by train—as our arrangements to go by car have broken down. It is very warm here: it will be much colder, we hear, up north. The Japanese air-raids here have been far from alarming, since we came: and anyhow we're living outside the town. Will write from Hankow if possible. Both well. Love to all. C.

Travel is very bad for the figure. We are both getting stouter. Wystan

March 16
Hankow

Both well. The weather has turned warmer and the snow all gone, here. I find H. never got the camera I sent.[6] Could you follow this up?

Will write more fully in three weeks, when we return to civilisation. Thank you for the cards. Best love. C.

April 5
Siam

Just to let you know that we're alive! We left Hankow about 3
weeks ago, went north by train to Chungchow, stayed there, then east
along the railway to Kwei The and Hsiu Chou, which is where the
line ends. There we went up and visited the front, which was interesting and not in the least dangerous, and thence returned, right along
the southern shore of the Yellow River to Siam. From there we hope
to get some sort of motor conveyance back south to Chungtu, and
so return along the Yangtzse, via Chungking, to Hankow. When we
reach there, I'll write of course. Also, we'll air mail some articles to the
*News Chronicle*, which, if they're published will give you some idea of
what we've seen. We're both quite well and much enjoying ourselves. I
really hope and think China is going to win this war. It is a marvellous
country—so enormous, untidy, varied and full of possibilities of every
kind. I can quite understand anybody settling here for life—but there
is one appalling obstacle: the language! I really believe that, if they're to
get anywhere, they'll have to adopt English as a means of communication, to bridge the dialect gulf.

The weather has been glorious, but is cloudy today. A very good
hotel here—much the best we've seen since Hongkong. We have collected masses of material—political, artistic, cultural. I am bringing you
some rubbings of engraved stones [here]—some of them are marvel-
lously beautiful.

We may not be in Hankow till the end of April—so expect a letter when you see me!

> Hope all is well.
> Best love,
> C.

April 21
[Cable from Hankow]

SEND ALL FUTURE MAIL CARE CURTBROWN NEWYORK INFORM
EVERYBODY=WYSTOPHER


April 21
The British Consulate
Hankow

My darling Mummy,

Thank you so much for the four letters I've just received, and for the cuttings, and for all your help in transacting business lately. I don't know what I would have done without you; and I certainly refuse to let the Group Theatre have you, they aren't worthy of such a secretary!

I wonder if you'll have got off to Ireland, or not? And, if so, whether you'll have had the cable I'm sending, asking you to forward all letters in future c/o of Curtis Brown. 18 East 48th Street. New York? The reason for this is that we've decided not to return to Hongkong at all. It so happens that the British Ambassador and his staff are going down there, and they will pick up our things and bring them up to Shanghai. Meanwhile, we shall leave here next week and go to Shanghai direct, overland to Ningpo, which is all in Chinese territory, and thence by boat across to the International Settlement. We shall stay in Shanghai about a week, and then probably leave direct for the States.

We have just finished a series of six articles on our experiences for the *News Chronicle,* which we are sending to *Harper's Bazaar.* They ought to be published about the middle of May, if the *Chronicle* accepts them; anyhow, they justify our claim to be journalists! We have lots of material: indeed, if we have to leave China tomorrow, we could still write the book.

Much interested in the reviews. I had expected a stab from Waugh sooner or later.[7] But the *Guardian* is terribly sniffy. I wonder if it'll sell, at all. Altogether, I'm afraid it is going to be a disappointment, financially. Lucky they took "Sally" in N. York.

How dreadful about Nanny. I am writing to her, of course.

I hope you won't find Limerick terribly upsetting. There are so many places, now, that I feel I could never bear to visit again; but perhaps the feeling wears off.

The Austrian business horrified us out here.[8] Indeed, it made our own visit to the Front seem very provincial, and safe, as indeed it was. Peter Fleming is here now, and off to the front tomorrow. I had to reassure his wife, who is very nice indeed, how unalarming it was. I trust you don't get bothered by all these air-raid reports. If you read that there's been an air-raid in Hankow, it means that some bombs were dropped about four miles away, on the air-field. The other night, I slept through a big raid, which only shows you that they aren't very terrible, and anyhow the moon is too small now to light them, till next month, when we'll be gone.

> Love from Wystan and much from
> myself to you both,
> C.

May 26
British Embassy
Shanghai

My darling Mummy,

Well, this notepaper says our most important bit of news—we got here yesterday, safe and well, on a boat from Wenchow. Our plans are to stay just as long as it takes to find a ship going to the U.S.A., and then set off.

I expect you got my cable safely, telling you to send everything in future c/o Curtis Brown. New York? And no doubt you told everybody? Mail still trickles through to us here, but only from people who wouldn't be likely to know.

We had a very interesting journey from Hankow to Kiukiang, Nanchang and Kinhwa. From Kinhwa (Kinghua, Chinghwa, Kinhwafu—it varies on every map) we went by car up to a placc called Tunki (never marked) where we met Peter Fleming and visited the South-Eastern front in his company—a real Fleming journey over the mountains, with ponies and chairs. The front was not very thrilling—we weren't allowed into the trenches, as the Japs were advancing: they moved into one town only 12 hours after we left it—but the trip was scenically beautiful and our companions most amusing. We both like Fleming extremely. He isn't anything at all resembling the author of his books—that infuriatingly modest well-bred Lucky Strike.

Here we are in the lap of luxury and surrounded by the kindness of the Clark Kerns, who must be about the nicest Ambassador and Ambassadress in the Service. Our only worry is about Europe. We missed one ghastly crisis—it seems—while hanging about in newsless Wenchow; but now another is brewing. The people here seem to have been quite resigned to a big flare-up, only a few days ago.

Thank you so much for your letters—forwarded from Hongkong. And resign yourself to a long wait before you hear again—remembering that we have now *definitely* finished with this Chinese war, and are running far fewer risks than you are, in Europe!

So glad Nanny is better. Hope that Ireland was a success?

Best love,
C.

June 25
On Board the Canadian Pacific Steamship
"Empress of Asia"

My darling Mummy,

This is just to tell you we hope to reach Southampton in the Britannic on or about July 14. What time we shall get to London, I can't say—but the steamship offices wd know, nearer the date.

A good but cold and very dull voyage across the northern Pacific—10 days without land! We reach Vancouver the day after tomorrow and shall be in N. York July 1st till the 9th. Hope post awaits me there.

Both well—trust you are, too.

Christopher

[Dover]
August 16
Tuesday

    Just to let you know Tony and I are going over to see Gerald today, returning Thursday.[9] I shall call for letters at East Cliff, then catch an afternoon train to town in time for concert.

                 Love,
                 C.

[early December]
Appt. 6
29 Rue de Stassart.
Brussels

    This is just to give you my new address. This is a very nice flat—nearly opposite the English Church! Wystan and I are busy finishing up the China book, etc. Please send all post here from now on.[10]

                 Love, C.

December 21
Appt. 6
29 Rue de Stassart.
Brussels

My darling Mummy,
 This is a Christmas letter, instead of a card, to wish you a happy
Christmas, or to wish, at any rate, that Christmas won't be more than
usually depressing. One can be glad at least that it won't be the first
war-Christmas, with fraternization in the trenches, and all the other
horrors of 1914. As for next year, a fortune-teller's assured me that I am
going to make a lot of money! She is the wife of the first secretary at the
Embassy here, and I must say, some of the things she told me were brilliant. For instance, she said: 'I see a capital letter in your hand. It's the
name of someone who has been of great importance in your life. The
name begins with an H.' Talking of Heinz, I am getting very worried
about him. He wasn't written, despite the various letters I've sent him.
I do hope he hasn't got into trouble for receiving money from abroad?
I suppose we shall hear, sooner or later. I enclose the *Harper's Bazaar*
article. It occurs to me that they have never paid me for it! Could you
communicate with them, and make sure? The address is on the cutting,
and I suppose the number is in the book? If they haven't yet sent the
money, please ask them to send it all to me, because I've already paid
Wystan his half, in advance. And would you please send me the cheque
here? I have had a financial blow. Curtis Brown of New York suddenly
wrote demanding forty pound: or so, which I owe them as the balance
of some money I borrowed in the summer. I'd thought, comfortably,
that my American royalties would cover it. But there haven't been any!
The snow is falling here, rather drearily, but it is warmer now that it's on
the ground. Wystan is much worse off than I am, because his hot-water
pipes have burst, and he sits writing sonnets in his overcoat—about

Brussels in winter! As I told you, Jacky Hewit is staying with me.[11] He enjoys cooking, which is a great comfort, and saves us both no end of money. I was hoping that Cuthbert Worsley would come out, but he hasn't.[12] No doubt the newspaper reports of gales in the Channel sounded too alarming. I still hope that Stephen and a party from Paris may arrive for the New Year. Would you ring up Stephen's flat and give him my address here? Though I doubt if he'll still be in town. Are you going away for Christmas, I wonder? And has R. decided to go up to Marple? I shall have to hold over my Xmas presents to the household until I get back. Nanny has never got her birthday present yet. Neither has R. Oh dear, oh dear. We see Gerald occasionally, but not often. On Saturday, we are invited to lunch with Salinger. He is very grand, nowadays, climbing higher and higher in the social scale. This year, he managed to get his wife presented at court. She went about all over Brussels talking about it, but unfortunately did not know that, in Belgian French, the word 'Cour' means not only 'Court' but also 'lavatory'. So you can imagine the misunderstandings which arose! This flat is really a great success, much the nicest I've ever had in this city. It is just the right size, and quite self-contained. Also, it's near to a very cheap shopping district, so one pays much less for provisions, and doesn't have to take so many trams and taxis. I told you, didn't I, that the China book is really finished at last? We decided to cut out the dialogue between Hongkong and Macao. Wystan wrote two more sonnets, instead. I'm afraid readers are going to get very little for their money.

My love to all the household, and much to yourself,

> ever your loving,
> Christopher

I never enquired about your tooth? I do hope it is better. What a horrid thing to happen!

George Washington Hotel
23rd St and Lexington Avenue.
N .Y. city.

March 10.

My darling Mummy,

Very many thanks for your letter. You are one of the very few who write, or whose letters ever reach me. I keep writing to you, but the mails get worse and worse. In future, it is best to find out what boat is sailing and put the name on the envelope. Or so I'm told.

We are still here, but hope to move into this apartment on the 1st of April. Meanwhile, it seems likely that Wystan will very soon go off to teach somewhere. He has lots of possibilities on hand. As for me, it is rather more difficult. I want, quite frankly, to be paid to do nothing ; so that I can settle down to write my books ! But nobody is likely to agree that it is in the interest of literature to support me !

Meanwhile, I potter around with odd jobs. Reviewing and suchlike. We meet fewer people. At least, I do. I am quite contented, but a bit restless. I'd like either to travel or settle down to work. I want to sink much more deeply into the life of this country. My real instinct is to go away by myself for a while. But I doubt if I shall.

Could you, please, send me two of the six copies of JOURNEY TO A WAR which you should get soon from Faber ? Because I doubt very much whether there will be any American edition till the autumn. GOODBYE TO BERLIN hasn't been reviewed yet. This weekend will start things off. I'll send you the cuttings when they arrive.

Am very well. And still confirmed in my anti-coffee-and-tea fad !

Love to everybody,

C.

# *1939*

During this momentous year, *Good-bye to Berlin* is published by the Hogarth Press in England and by Random House in the United States, and *Journey to a War* comes out from Faber and Faber. Auden and Isherwood sail for New York in January. The Republicans surrender in Spain, ending the Spanish civil war, and Hitler divides the remainder of Czechoslovakia. Germany invades Poland on September 1, and England declares war on Germany two days later. Isherwood is unhappy in New York; Auden seems at home immediately. In May, Isherwood leaves New York for California. He and a young American he calls Harvey Young in the letters (in other writings known as Vernon Old) take a bus across the country and settle in Hollywood. Isherwood quickly takes to life in Southern California, becoming interested in Yoga, meditation, and the teachings of Swami Prabhavananda. He becomes a permanent resident of the United States and gets his first filmwriting job at Goldwyn Studios. Despite having difficulty with his own writing, he spends the latter half of the year immersing himself in Southern California culture, meditating, working for Goldwyn, and anxiously fretting over the safety of Richard and Kathleen back in England.

January 29
Hotel Taft
New Haven, Connecticut

My darling Mummy,

This is just a line to tell you that we finally arrived—after the most awful voyage. Three big storms, and the bows quite covered in ice.

We have found a nice hotel—the George Washington—23rd St and Lexington Ave. But just at the moment we're visiting a friend of Wystan's at Yale. We are off again on Monday to Princeton to see Thomas Mann.[1]

Meanwhile, we are beginning to rewrite *Dogskin*.

I'll write again in a few days.

Love to all,
C.


February 7
George Washington Hotel
23rd Street and Lexington Avenue
New York City

My darling Mummy,

Your letter has just arrived today. There was some extra delay, because Random House isn't open on Saturdays or Sundays.

Maybe in future you had better write and send all my mail direct here.

I am sorry I didn't write you more fully in my first letter, but I was in a room with people talking and there was very little time. Also, I didn't really have much news. After a fortnight in this country, nearly, there is, alas, no sensational business deal to report. Indeed, our play shows very little promise of being put on; not because nobody is interested, but because everybody is interested in the wrong way. They want very childish alterations, which would increase the topical value of the production for one week after writing them, and would be hopelessly out of date in a fortnight, since history moves so fast nowadays.

We are spending money at an altogether fabulous rate. A dollar, which costs about four and threepence to buy, has the purchasing power of barely half a crown. This hotel isn't expensive, certainly, by London standards; but in London I don't live in an hotel! Incidentally, the manager, who is very kind by nature, comes from Manchester and used to spend a lot of time in Mellor! So he is extra nice to us.

Wystan is so angry about the newspaper cutting in the *Daily Express* that, after consulting with Erika Mann, he has written to his lawyer in England with a view to possible proceedings.[2] I call it simply disgusting to print such things. If, by any chance, journalists try to get anything from you about the whole business, you will, I know, refuse to make a statement.

The poem by Mr Callam is certainly a coughdrop.[3] I'll write to him sometime. I hope he doesn't bother you any more.

We are both worried about the European situation. The American papers make it sound most alarming. And the President's wobbling won't help matters. If he would only promise to fight with England and France, then war would be impossible; but of course he daren't do this for home political reasons. It is very difficult to say what the mass of people in this country really want him to do. They are certainly violently pacifist, and probably inclined to let Europe blow itself up. But they are very scared to German influence in Mexico and S. America, and realize that a war might involve Canada, so it's on their own doorstep, after all.

This is a very grim city in wintertime. So much of it is slum, or near-slum. Many of the streets are strikingly like Manchester, or Camden Town. And you often get the feeling that the skyscrapers are wicked, blasphemous, like the Tower of Babel. All the same, in its own way, it is very beautiful. And I would love being here, if only we could leave this hotel life and have an apartment. We both miss Brussels, and Jacky, very much indeed.[4]

We spent a nice time in Princeton, visiting Thomas Mann. Princeton is really charming, much more attractive than Yale. It is just a large village of wooden houses in the old colonial style, and looked delightful in the snow. Thomas was very nice. So was his wife. And Erika and Klaus were there too.

I don't know what we shall do next. Chris Wood writes from Hollywood begging us to join him.[5] It would certainly be warmer. This city is under snow again today, although it isn't very cold. Wystan is busy writing a poem about the death of W. B. Yeats. I am trying to start my novel, but it's a bit sticky.

Did that boy from next door ever return my books? I hope so.

Did you hear the sensational news, which I believe I forgot to tell you in my last letter, and which I myself only was told as we were getting into the boat-train, that Salinger has been arrested? It was in connection with that Dr Imianitoff I spoke to you about.[6] It seems that they had done a lot of business together. Maybe you read it in the English papers. Perhaps by this time he has been released again. Gerald, so I heard today from Jacky, simply daren't return to Brussels in consequence.

Well, that's all for now. The Manhattan sails tomorrow, and I hope this letter will go with her.

All my love, and to R. Tell Nanny I am very sorry about her brother.

C.

[New York]
February 1939

The tickets were a *present* from Kearsey—so you can't possibly be asked to pay for them.[7] He sent me a voucher which entitled me to 15/- worth of tickets. Am hoping to have a longer letter from you by this mail. We are thinking of moving into an apartment. Both well.

Love to all. C.

February 28
George Washington Hotel
Twenty-Third Street and Lexington Avenue
New York City

My darling Mummy,

Thank you so much for sending on the cuttings, and describing the performances of *On the Frontier*. Nobody else bothered to do so, except Jacky Hewit—who didn't care much for the way it was produced.[8]

I gather that it has little or no chance of being put on for a run? I only hope that *Goodbye to Berlin* and the China book will do better.

We live in the midst of permanent war-scare. I think the Americans are much more pessimistic than the Europeans—chiefly because they fear to be involved; which the Europeans *know* they'll be involved, anyway. We get very depressed, reading the papers. The Germans, we are told, would destroy London in 24 hours. So mind you leave, the moment things begin to look nasty!

The fear of a crisis keeps our plans vague, too. There's no point in going to Hollywood if we have to come racing home again. For the moment we'll stay in this hotel, and probably move into our apartment on April 1. We have found a very nice one, at a reasonable rent—80 dollars a month.

Wystan is very busy writing articles and poems. I am trying to do a story for *Red Book Magazine,* which if accepted, would be worth 400 dollars. 4!

We see comparatively few people. There is the Mann family, of course. And a young American named Lincoln Kirstein, who is a friend of Stephen's.[9] He runs a ballet company, with which he tours the country. He is very intelligent and tells us a great deal about the U.S.A.

The weather here is very variable. It never does anything for more than one day, and the temperature fluctuates wildly. But so far neither of us has caught cold. Wystan continues to exclaim against the food. I rather like it. I feel much better now that I've entirely given up coffee and tea in favour of orange-juice and milk!

Random House are publishing *Goodbye to Berlin* this week. I am hoping for good notices. But the American market is most unsatisfactory for novels. The *average* sale is far lower than in England—although best-sellers and film-scripts get paid fantastically. Also, publishers are less honest, I think.

The Americans want everything canned. They want digests of books, selections of music, bits of plays. Their interest is hard to hold for long. No great reputation is safe. Everybody is constantly being reconsidered. This is partly good, of course. But there is a lot of cruelty in the publisher's attitude toward has-beens. The radio is nearly impossible to listen to, because of constant advertising interruptions.

I must stop—to catch the mail.

<blockquote>
Love to all—<br>
ever your loving<br>
C.
</blockquote>

March 10
George Washington Hotel
23rd St and Lexington Avenue
N.Y. city

My darling Mummy,

Very many thanks for your letter. You are one of the very few who write, or whose letters ever reach me. I keep writing to you, but the mails get worse and worse. In future, it is best to find out what boat is sailing and put the name on the envelope. Or so I'm told.

We are still here, but hope to move into this apartment on the 1st of April. Meanwhile, it seems likely that Wystan will very soon go off to teach somewhere. He has lots of possibilities on hand. As for me, it is rather more difficult. I want, quite frankly, to be paid to do nothing; so that I can settle down to write my books! But nobody is likely to agree that it is in the interest of literature to support me!

Meanwhile, I potter around with odd jobs. Reviewing and such-

like. We meet fewer people. At least, I do. I am quite contented, but a
bit restless. I'd like either to travel or settle down to work. I want to sink
much more deeply into the life of this country. My real instinct is to go
away by myself for a while. But I doubt if I shall.

Could you, please, send me two of the six copies of *Journey to a
War* which you should get soon from Faber? Because I doubt very much
whether there will be any American edition till the autumn. *Goodbye to
Berlin* hasn't been reviewed yet. This weekend will start things off. I'll
send you the cuttings when they arrive.

Am very well. And still confirmed in my anti-coffee-and-tea fad!

Love to everybody,
C.


March 26
George Washington Hotel

My darling Mummy,

Thank you for your letter and all the cuttings you've sent. I am so
sorry to hear about your foot. I do hope it is better now? I was beginning to be worried, as I hadn't heard from you for some time. And I
might well worry about all my other friends, except that I know they
can't simply have died. Hardly anybody has written; not even Morgan
or Stephen.[10] We feel very much isolated!

By this time you will have had a cable from me, asking you to
get Wystan's and my birth-certificate from Somerset House. This is
because we want to get on to the quota: i.e. obtain permission to work
in this country. Journalism is permitted, but Wystan will soon take up a
school-job, and this, without a quota-visa, is illegal.

Meanwhile, we are going to move into our apartment at the end of the week. The address will be 237 East 81st Street. New York City. But all letters to the George Washington will reach us, anyhow.

You are quite right in feeling that I am restless and ill at ease in New York. Maybe I shall never settle down to work in this city. But I think our time here has been very valuable. Not only have I learnt a great deal about American life, but I have thought over a number of things, and revised my ideas considerably. I think we are both rapidly becoming less political, and considerably more definitely pacifist. I can no longer believe in war to stop Hitler. Hitler (what he stands for) won't ever be stopped by another war; even if England wins it. There will just be a 1918 peace, twenty years of preparation, and then off we go again. There was a time, perhaps, when we still had something really worth fighting for. Now, there are merely our colonies. I still think, if war breaks out, that we shall come back; but only to share the suffering. Neither of us will fight. No doubt this attitude is rather futile, since, when you are being bombed, it doesn't matter whether you 'resist' or not. But it is how I feel.

I wish you were over here, and Richard, too, though I doubt whether you'd like it much. There is a tremendous amount of sheer natural suspicion between the English and Americans, and so few people are strong or patient enough to overcome it. I hope to, of course; but sometimes doubt if I can. One thing I want very much to do, if possible. To go right across America, slowly, either by bus, or getting rides from motorists, to the Pacific. I think I'll do this in May. Christopher Wood is anxious that I shall. He's still in Hollywood, and could, of course, be a great help with introductions, etc.

I have done some reviewing, but can settle to no serious work. Perhaps I must just wait. But I keep trying.

Our money affairs are always on the verge of collapse, but there is always some new pittance which saves us from final disaster. Most

of the people in this town seem to be living about a mile beyond their
incomes, so perhaps we are getting the correct American attitude to life!

I am very glad that *Goodbye to Berlin* has had a success in
England. Here, it certainly hasn't; though various people who read it
were full of praise. I think it is an honest piece of work, as far as it goes.
I wish I could write novels, real ones, but perhaps I can't. Maybe I have
come to the limit of my talent, and shall just go on being 'promising'
until people are tired of me; but it won't come out. I could describe
anybody, anything, in the world; but I can't make it all into a pattern.
Perhaps that is the penalty you pay for not believing in anything posi-
tive. Perhaps it's a certain lack of vitality. Perhaps it's only New York.
Wystan, on the other hand, flourishes exceedingly. Never has he written
so much. And he seems to be formulating his ideas, and making the
most impressive speeches. He is out a great deal.

About business. I had a letter from Curtis Brown, saying they
enclosed a cheque for £ 1. 13. 8d. They didn't. They also didn't send the
income-tax payment slip, which I must have, to prove the tax was paid.
Would you ring them about it? The letter was signed by Miss Sonia
Chapter, of the translation department, as the money was from the
Polish version of *Mr Norris*. The cheque had better be paid straight into
my account at the bank. And, while you are at the bank, could you tell
them that Heinz's new address is Berlin-Neukolln. Zietenstrasse 37. vorn
3 Treppen. I have just heard that he's moved. Poor thing, he ruptured
himself at work, and must now have an operation. My only consolation
is that he'll certainly have some kind of exemption from the army, and
only have to do light work in consequence.[11]

The other business is a letter from the agent, Walter Peacock.
60 Haymarket. SW 1 (Whitehall 9186) who writes that he has the
sum of £ 5. 15. 11d. for amateur performances of *On the Frontier* in
Manchester, and asks do Wystan and I want it divided equally. Of
course we do. Could you please tell him this, and collect, and pay into

my account, the money? If it isn't too much trouble, could you note these two payments in the cash-book in my desk (top drawer)? Then everything will be quite clear when I have to make another income-tax statement.

Louis Macneice has arrived here to lecture, and is staying in this hotel.[12] I am looking forward to getting copies of *Journey to a War* and the reviews. They made an idiotic misprint. On the tops of all the pages of the Travel-Diary, they printed Hongkong-Macao, which is sheer nonsense. If you are feeling in a belligerent mood, perhaps you'd ring Fabers' and tell them we are both amazed at this carelessness, and ask how it can have happened. If possible, try to speak to Mr de la Mare. He is the most unpleasant of them.

No more news for the present. So will close.

Much love to all.
Your loving son,
C.

Has anything more been heard of Cape's Traveller's Library edition of *All the Conspirators*? I still have not seen Cyril Connolly's introduction, and would much like to.

April 20
237 East 81st Street
New York City

My darling Mummy,

Very many thanks for your several letters and the press-cuttings you've sent me from time to time. It is nice to see that the two books have been appreciated. I should really be writing this letter to Richard, in reply to his. But I see from your last that he has gone up to Marple, and so perhaps it'll be better if you send this on to him instead, so's you'll both have news. I was astounded at the neatness of the typing and can well imagine that a long letter like that must have taken hours to write.[13] At first, it seems more like etching than writing, it's so slow. You ask how quickly I type myself. Well, I'll see. Meanwhile here is the cutting from the *Life* which you may or may not have seen. It appeared last week. The picture of Erika is very good.[14] (I timed myself just now, and find that I only did thirty words in a minute. I believe I can type much faster than this when I am copying.)

Our time at the apartment is nearly up. I hope to get off on my western tour some time during the first week in May. Wystan will start his teaching then. Of course, Hitler may still do something unpleasant between then and now; but even if war breaks out I may possibly decide to go to California for a short time. It will be very difficult to return right away, in any case; as I expect all traffic would be completely disorganized. I am glad R. has this possibility of working at Marple. It sounds much safer. Mind you and the others go *straight* to Penmaenmawr.[15] And please try to take my diaries, and the papers in the bottom drawer of the bureau (or some of them) with you! They still contain lots of material I want to try to write up, some day. However, don't let's be too pessimistic. Like the Coming of the Lamb of God, war is sure to arrive when least expected. And just now everybody is waiting for it. I have a great deal of faith in the essential wrongness of all mass-opinions on these subjects.

I haven't altogether liked this flat. It is so dark, and somehow still belongs too obviously to its owner. But we have a very efficient coloured maid, and can have our evening meal at home, which is nice. I am doing quite a lot of reviewing for the *New Republic,* which corresponds to the *New Statesman,* over here, and gradually getting to

know the work of the American novelists. Many of them write wonderfully, but there is so little form. They just take great chunks of life; and
the story never ends for any reason except that the author is tired. On
Sunday, there is a studio production of *F6*. We have rewritten the ending, and now I really believe that we have found the solution to all our
difficulties with it. It is far less obscure and more theatrically effective.

Now I must end, to catch the Queen Mary. Louis Macneice is
returning in her, and I have asked him to come and see you, to tell you
all our minor news. I hope he will. If he doesn't telephone, perhaps
you'll ring him up.

Lots of love to you both,

always your loving
C.

May 4
237 E. 81st Street
N.Y. City

My darling Mummy,

This is just to say that, all being well, I'm off, the day after
tomorrow, on my long bus journey. The first stop will be Washington,
where I hope to spend two or maybe three days. I'll send you post-cards
enroute.

One of my American friends, Harvey Young, is coming with me;
so I'll be in the real native atmosphere, right from the start.[16]

Two business points: Durrants have sent me a bill. Would you
please pay it, and continue my subscription? I have enough in the Bank,
right now, to fix that. And would you continue the payments I am

making to Heinz? I forget if I already asked you about this. In the normal way, they would lapse in June. The Bank knows all the details. I have just met Ford Maddox Ford, who is a mixture of Grandad, and Wystan as he might be at the age of seventy.[17] It is difficult to see him as the fatal seducer who wrecked so many lives! His present wife is French, and very nice.

As I think I told you already, please write c/o Christopher Wood. 8766 Arlene Terrace. Hollywood. California. The other addresses will be forwarded, but not so quickly.

The world situation seems worse than ever; and people here are talking of a German-Russian lineup. But I've got a bit tired of worrying; and have decided not to do so until the next crisis arrives—tomorrow, probably!

I love Richard's letters. He must be improving his typing very rapidly.

All my love,
C.

May 19
Grand Canyon

This card gives you no idea whatever of what the Canyon is like—but an ordinary photograph gives still less, because the colours are extraordinary. We have been spending the day here. Tomorrow we leave for California and should arrive the day after in Los Angeles.

Love, C.

May 23
8766 Arlene Terrace
Hollywood, Calif.


My darling Mummy,

Well, we got here—after crossing several hundred more miles of Arizona and California—and I found your two letters. Looking back on the journey, I liked Washington and New Orleans best—but the desert is perhaps the most wonderful experience. I am trying to write something about it.

Hollywood is a great sprawling, dazzling new place—like a World's Fair—but it's wonderful to be here, in the sunshine, among the eucalyptus trees and the subtropical birds. How I love the sun. I feel as if we'd arisen from the tomb—full of energy and gaiety. We have taken a 2-room apartment, very cheap, with every convenience. The people are most friendly. They address you as 'Love' and 'Honey'. There is less privacy than at a public school—but also less criticism. We all live openly, in the great eye of the sunshine—and if you appear dressed in red velvet, leading a baby puma nobody bats an eyelid.

My money affairs are in the last stages of ruin—but I am looking round for a job—and Chris Wood is prepared to lend me enough to see us through. He is very kind, and so is Gerald Heard, who has grown a beard, and now so strongly resembles Christ that I feel like Mary Magdalene.[18] Viertel is expected very shortly, and I hope he will find me some work.[19] Meanwhile, I am restarting my novel.

Wystan is teaching, near New York—as I think I told you.

Will you please ask the Westminster Bank manager to write me a letter, saying that I have an account at his bank? He needn't say how much is in it! Just that I have had an account there for so and so long.

The immigration authorities want this—so it should be sent off as soon as possible.

Will write again later. Hope you passed the Red + exam.

Best love,
Christopher

June 7
6406 Franklin Avenue
Hollywood, Cal.

My darling Mummy,

Just to let you know that things are still going quite well here. That is to say, the sun continues to shine, and I am still happy and in excellent health. I love your and Richard's joint letter. Is R. good enough to take dictation? He seems to have progressed wonderfully quickly.

No prospect, definitely, of a job yet. But Mrs Viertel, with whom I had dinner the other day, talked about the possibility of my working on the Madame Curie film for Garbo.[20] Of course, this film has been written already, chiefly by Aldous Huxley, whom I met. He is nice, but very vague and remote. A wonderful woman here is curing his sight by exercises. He was nearly blind in one eye. Now he can catch balls, and read with it.[21] Berthold is still in New York, and may not come here till July, which is a pity.

You will be amazed to hear that I am becoming very much pre-occupied with Yoga. It seems to run in the Isherwood family![22] Gerald Heard has just written a most remarkable book about it, which will be published soon. I used to despise Yoga because I thought it was just a search for personal salvation, without any reference to society—but Gerald makes you see how vitally necessary it is to organize some mass 'change of heart', if mankind is ever to get out of this horrible mess. The Communists' mistake is to assume that people will automatically get perfect if the social system is changed. Certainly they will get better, but not much, because the old hatreds and ambitions will remain. The new Yoga philosophy is much more radical. It really aims at carrying on human evolution one more step, and giving mankind new psychic powers to match the powers conferred by science and mechanical inventions. Without such powers, we can never use our machines. They will use *us,* and, ultimately, destroy us.

On Monday, I hope, I am going into Mexico to get the quota visa. It is being arranged by a lady lawyer here (*not* a Salinger!) who specialises in such cases, and is a descendent of Napoleon! Her name is actually Miss Buonaparte. If all goes well, I shall only be away two or three days.

Wystan writes very happily from New York. He is through with his school, and proposes shortly to take a holiday. He will go to Taos in New Mexico, where D. H. Lawrence lived for a time. (He describes it in the story 'St. Mawr'.) Wystan has bought, or been given, a car.

Which reminds me that I have a car, too! It was absolutely necessary to buy one, if I am ever to have any work, because the distances here are enormous. Los Angeles, Hollywood and Santa Monica form one enormous garden city. In area, it must be nearly as big as London. In this country, the second hand car market is very highly organized, and you get very good bargains. This one is a Ford. Not very beautiful, but it goes.

I've just heard from Henry that he paid £25 into my account.[23] I should think, by this time, that a certain amount of other money will have accumulated there. Could you let me have £30, please, in notes? And, as you can draw cheques, pay your self back right away.

Hope you both passed your Red + tests all right.

Was *All the Conspirators* ever published? I'd love see a copy.

This must be all, for now. Very much love to you both.


Write again soon.

Christopher



June 18

6406 Franklin Avenue

Hollywood, Cal.


My darling Mummy,

Just got your postcard, and the cuttings. I wish people wouldn't say we are callous about China—because we really weren't.[24] And I do think this shows through, if you read the book fair-mindedly.

Well, I went to Mexico and got my quota visa, without fuss. The place I went to—to see the American Consul—was Ensenada, down that peninsula which runs out from California. What a beautiful country this is! I do wish you could be here—out of reach of the bombing planes.

We have just rented a small house, high up the hill, overlooking the valley. The garden is full of humming birds. If it weren't for outside worries, I think one could be happy in this place for ever and ever.

If there is no war, I hope to return to England in the late autumn—provided I can afford to! I must now make a big drive to get a job.

Harvey Young is an art student—very serious, rather German in appearance and mentality (his ancestry is English and South German) not unlike Heinz. I first met him last summer, when we were in New York. He believes in diet, exercises, and likes reading Roman history.

He is a great admirer of Gerald Heard. He is very fond of horses and snakes. Extremely good-natured. Inclined to fat. Wystan likes him. In fact, everybody likes him. Alas, he is not a very good cook! I think his drawing shows promise.

My own work is still hanging fire. But when we get settled down, I'll begin something. At this moment, I'm still so preoccupied with Yoga—reading about it, thinking about it, wondering if it is the right way. All I know, definitely, is that I have stopped hating—or nearly stopped. So I can't remain in any Anti front—the anti-fascists, the anti-nazis, or even the anti-Chamberlains. 'Liberty or Death' is simply meaningless rubbish—because the next war will not be fought for Liberty. And 'Appeasement' is no good, either—because it's not genuine friendliness—only throwing sops to an angry dog, instead of going up to it fearlessly and holding out your hand. It is no use blaming Chamberlain at Munich.[25] He could never have handled Hitler, because Hitler is a mystic, and could only be dealt with by another mystic. If the Church of England were a live religion, the right person to send would have been the Archbishop of Canterbury. The absurdity of this last statement is just a measure of how far we have fallen.

I shall never become a real Yogin myself—but I do believe that I am on the right path—and that, if I live through this epoch, I will be able to get somewhere, and tell people the way. Being a writer helps a lot. But we all misuse the powers we've developed. I wish I knew why Jack gave it up.[26] Probably because Cyril Scott was a fake, and so he became disgusted.[27] It is so dangerous to pin your faith on people, not ideas. When the person fails, the idea remains—but one can't see that, in the first disappointment. That is why people who discover that Stalin is a bloodthirsty tyrant so often conclude that Communism is nonsense.

In our arguments, I used to maintain that when Socialism was established, people would become better. So they would—up to a point. But you were perfectly right in retorting that everything would lapse back into the old abuses, because 'you can't change Human Nature'. I got angry, because, in my heart, I agreed with you. Now I see that we were both wrong. Human nature *could* be changed, but not through Socialism. Yoga, brought up to date to fit Western requirements, is the only way out. But people *may* refuse to take it. If so, we shall cease to evolve, and mankind will harden into a species with limited powers and functions, like the ant or the shark.

Better go on writing to this, or Chris Wood's address for the present. I get all the mail. Very much love to all at home. Your loving,

C.

July 8
7136 Sycamore Trail
Hollywood, California

My darling Mummy,

Thank you for the two letters, postcard and press cuttings just received. I have written to Berger.[28] (Incidentally, his address seems to be Villa Candens, not Campden.) I had a letter from him today, in which he said he might be coming out here, in which case maybe I could work with him after all. But it's just as well I'm not in London right now, as he remarks casually how nice it would be for me to translate his Baconian novel. As I know from hearing it read, it's immensely long!

How too bad that Richard didn't pass the examination.[29] Evidently we are neither of us medically gifted![30] But I'm glad you got through all right yourself. I do hope you won't ever have occasion to use your knowledge. As I write this the crisis seems in a momentary lull. No doubt it'll have boiled over again by the time the German harvest is in, and you get this. Of all the futile things to fight about, Danzig seems the silliest. Perhaps if the commission had listened to Basil Fry history would have been different![31] He had his own solution I remember. But have no idea what it was. In those days, such subjects merely bored me—only ten years ago!

If only you were all safe here. It is such a wonderful country. The mountains from my window look unbelievable in the sunset; and the woods round the house are full of humming-birds and blue jays. People come here from all over the United States, in order to live an extra ten years: the air is so wonderful. Of course, it is a very tragic country, too: like all promised lands. There have been a perpetual series of Gold Rushes out here—rushes for land, rushes for gold itself, rushes for the movies. Always the state is getting overcrowded; always there are outbursts of the most horrible violence—lynchings, strikes broken up with machine-guns and gas, evictions. At present, there is a trek going on from the Middle West. The farmers in the mid-western states have exhausted [the] land. It just won't yield any more, without fertilizers which they haven't the money to buy. They have borrowed from the big banks and now the agents of the banks are driving them off their land because they can't pay the interest. The banks are turning the land into huge cotton-farms. And when these fail, as they must, it will be sold for residential purposes to retiring tradesmen form the East Coast. So the farmers trek to California, hoping to find work in the fruit-picking. But the fruit-picking is only seasonal anyway, and there is such a surplus of labour that wages have gone down to nearly nothing. So great bands of nearly starving men and women roam about the state. And of course, they sometimes steal, and the residents are frightened of them, and drive them away with armed bands of auxiliary police. It's all such a mess.

I have no work yet, but I hope Viertel will find me some. He arrives today. People talk about the depression having hit the movies, but there is plenty of production going forward in the studios. Laughton has just arrived to make *The Hunchback of Notre Dame*.[32]

The cutting from the *Evening Standard* is certainly very ill-natured and quite untrue. We certainly never quarrelled with the New York intellectuals.[33] We were as nice as pie. Too nice. But these things are best ignored, I suppose.

Yes, Harvey Young is still with me. Klaus Mann is coming out soon. Wystan is somewhere in New Mexico, but won't come further, I think.

I enclose the contract. Yes, I got *All the Conspirators*. It looks nice, doesn't it?

Am stuck in my writing again, but not hopelessly: just biding my time. The novel just won't jell. It must wait.

Best love to you all,

C.

P.S. I see I have left some questions unanswered.

The quota is *absolutely* legal! It gives one the right to work in the U.S.A. and is therefore essential if you are meaning to get a job in the movies, where employment is very public, often the subject of newspaper comment, so that the authorities always find you out. I gather that the Mexicans required a slight encouragement to permit me to enter Mexico, in order to return with the visa. But that has nothing to do with the U.S.A. and is customary, and only cost about five pounds!

Salinger got 4½ years. I can't help feeling sorry, even if he was all we feared, and worse.

I see from a press clipping that there is an ending to *F.6.* which takes place in Broadcasting House, I certainly never wrote this. Wystan may have done so at the last moment. Or it may have been an invention of Doone's. Or just inaccurate. Please tell me exactly what happens.

The scenery of *Stagecoach* was shot in an Indian reservation near the Grand Canyon. We didn't actually pass through that country, but it was similar. Isn't it magnificent? I liked the film, too.

I had seen Connolly's preface already in proof. It is quite good, I think, but too complimentary. I don't think they should have had one at all. Rereading the book, I don't find it so bad. But it is very young and very 'period'.

The money from the Westminster hasn't arrived yet. But no doubt it will. You might, however, send me the name of the Westminster Bank's agent, as a precaution.*

Very sorry to hear about Mr Bury—if you are sorry.


*money just arrived.



July 17
7136 Sycamore Trail
Hollywood, California

My darling Mummy,

Thank you for your letter. I hate to think of you in London, waiting for the war. Wouldn't it be better to move to Penmaenmawr? Of course, as you say, it mayn't come for some time yet. But I shouldn't like you to be in the first air-raid, which will probably be much the worst, as the English are certain to have mismanaged all the precautions. They invariably do, at the beginning of a war. Personally, I don't think Hitler will attack England completely without warning. Why should he? He still has a chance of persuading the British Government to keep out of it; and he would gain very little by surprise, now that the air-force and army is mobilized, anyway. I think there will probably be a fairly prolonged period of crisis, right after the harvest, leading either to war or to another postponement. Despite all Chamberlain's speeches, he doesn't say he'd automatically go to war if Danzig declared itself part of Germany. So there will be hasty negotiations with the Poles, and probably pressure put on them not to fight. Delay, in any case.

About my papers. I really don't much like the Bank having them. If you can't take them with you, perhaps they should be burnt, though I should regret that very much, as they contain a lot of material, still, which I may use one day. I would suggest your posting the other papers, including the larger, flat, dark green (?) diary, out here. But so many of the papers are not really worth preserving that I prefer to let them all take their chance. Couldn't you put all my papers and diaries in a locked suitcase and send them to Rachel at Wyberslegh, next time R. goes there?[34] Rachel would look after them, and then they wouldn't be a nuisance to you, If you did have to move quickly.

No. Harvey doesn't keep snakes! I wouldn't let him, anyway. I can't bear them, either. So don't let that deter you from coming to see us. If you came to New York, I'd come across to meet you there. But the journey is expensive, I'm afraid. I do wish you would both come.

Guy Burgess has appealed to me to help Jacky Hewit, who has a wonderful chance of getting a really good job in the hotel business, if he has the necessary training.[35] It means putting up a £50 bond, which will be returned. I don't know how much money I have in the Bank, but I would like him to have it. The rest I can pay later. The point is that I don't want Jacky to know the money came from me. So will you please communicate with Guy and give him a cheque for the amount I have at present. His address is 38 Chester Square (Sloane 4847). If he isn't in town, Anthony Blunt, his friend, will do as well.[36] Address: 30 Palace Court. W.2. Bay 0996.

> I'll write again soon.
> Best love,
> C.

August 8
7136 Sycamore Trail
Hollywood, California

My darling Mummy,

Thank you and Richard for the letter. How quickly can he write now? It is very satisfactory, being able to type like this.

I'm afraid it is rather a long time since you heard from me. The days go by very quickly, and I am apt to sit down to letter-writing only in fits: it is very difficult to keep answering the post as it arrives. You will have heard in my last letter that the money arrived safely here; and now I must thank you for arranging things with Jacky. I was a little surprised, myself, that he knew all about it, and extremely surprised when he rang me up! It must have cost between four and five pounds, at the very least. But no doubt, being on the switchboard at the Goring, he got special facilities. The voice was absolutely clear, in spite of the fact that there is a wireless link in the connection. One might as well have been speaking to someone here in Hollywood. Just in case anything catastrophic happens, and *you* ever want to call me, the number is Granite 9223. (Los Angeles has a large number of different exchanges, like London. I suppose you would have to say: 'Los Angeles—Granite' when you asked for it.)

It is very difficult for us to judge what is really happening in Europe. The newspapers here are provincial, alarmist and vague. At present, all their headlines are devoted to the gambling ships which are anchored off the coast, outside the three-mile limit. These ships have been declared illegal, and are in a state of semi-siege. Customers were taken out to them in special motor-boats to play roulette, etc, and they did such an enormous business that they could afford to employ aviators to write smoke advertisements over the city! The *New York Times,* which is the best newspaper, probably, in the world, arrives late and is tiresome to get. The radio news bulletins, like all other programmes, are commercially sponsored, and so constantly interrupted by advertising announcements that you lose patience listening to them. (You probably know that in the U.S.A. the air belongs to a number of independent stations, who sell their hours to various firms. These firms put on programmes, just like English programmes, but they are obliged to use some part of each hour advertising their products, as this is the only way in which they can make money out of the whole business. Radio listeners don't have to pay any kind of tax.)

Viertel is here, getting very restive for Europe. His desire to see Beatrix again is clothed in a political robe.[37] He feels he cannot be 'out of things'. Beatrix is seldom mentioned by name; she has become 'democracy' and 'the defence of culture'. Poor old thing, he gets terribly upset, and I soothe him as best I can. Whether our film will ever come to anything is still doubtful. The people in New York are very elusive when it's a question of paying down any money. Meanwhile, John van Druten, whom I like very much, as been trying to help me.[38] He has got me another agent. I hope she will be better than the last. He himself is doing a script on the 'Raffles' books.

I have met no big film stars except Charlie Chaplin, who was at lunch one day with Aldous Huxley. He is a charming, lively, white-haired little man, who alternates, I should imagine, between extremes of public high spirits and private depression. He acted a lot of his new film for us (he can talk of nothing else) about Hitler. Hitler will speak a nonsense language, based on the sound of German.[39] I think it will be very funny—if Hitler is still a laughing matter by the time it is produced!

I am very interested in what you say about Jack and Yoga.[40] Of course, the extreme forms of it are beyond the reach of the West, and, indeed, far beyond the reach of ordinary people anywhere. But you don't need to be Weissmuller in order to swim:[41] there are degrees of proficiency which anybody can attain to. The general public has been led to believe that Yoga is just tricks: being able to read thoughts, or stop your heart beating at will. But these powers are quite beside the point. If you suddenly find you have them, it means you have reached a certain stage of development, that is all. In fact, the powers are a terrible delusion and temptation for those who acquire them because they could be used for any purpose whatsoever. No, the real object, or rather, the *immediate* object of Yoga is to *overcome* greed, fear, the tyranny of possessions, vanity, etc etc. And to give you a permanent sense of calm and acceptance of whatever may come. This acceptance is so difficult, because it isn't mere fatalism or passive resignation. It is an inner ring of defence which cannot be broken down. Actually, the Yogic experience, in a very diluted and confused form, is familiar to any artist. You go through it when you are planning a novel, and have to put yourself into each of the characters, and accept and understand them for what they are. A painter puts himself into a landscape in the same way, and becomes, for the moment, part of the landscape, and feels that the landscape is part of himself. This experience is a source of goodwill towards everybody and everything which goes far deeper than mere kindness, or sympathy, or even love. Just as a scientist studying a dog goes far deeper than a sentimentalist who merely 'loves' the dog without trying to understand it.

This is what Yoga is, in essence. Nothing mysterious. Nothing
you need to read a lot of books about. In fact, you are strongly advised
not to read too many books, but to find a teacher (a trainer, really) who
will give you practical hints on how to spend these periods of meditation, or concentration, or whatever you like to call them. At present, I
am just doing an hour a day. Half in the morning, half in the evening.
There is an Indian here, who is training Gerald Heard, and I have been
to see him.[42] There are no physical exercises, at present. Later, you do
some very simple breathing, not much else. The Indian is very gay,
rather like a Chinese. He giggles the whole time. I had to ask him not
to talk about 'God', as the word has bad associations for me. So he
calls it 'the Self'. Yoga insists that it is absolutely immaterial what you
believe. If you think there is a personal God, you approach the subject
from another angle, that's all.

Would you like this place? I'm afraid that there's no social life to
offer you, as in Portugal. At least, I have none. I know very few people.
It seems hardly necessary, when you can talk to anybody, anywhere.
'Hi ya, Buddy?' says a perfectly strange man, who has come about the
gas. 'How's business?' The owner of the nearest garage was calling me
Chris before I'd been there twice. You would be treated more respect-
fully, of course; but all the ladies would probably behave like Thea
Mitchell.[43] The friend of the friends are friends. Actually, there must be
a huge English colony here. In fact, there is a huge colony of any race
you happen to look for. One's English accent is generally remarked on
at once, and frequently described as 'cute'. Americans are still on the
defensive against the English, being afraid the English will snub them.
I am bound to say they are often right.

The house is furnished with plain unpainted chairs and tables,
which we have waxed to keep them clean. We have goldfish and a par-
rot, a very small one, which likes to sit on your shoulder. There are two
living-rooms, a bedroom, a bathroom and kitchen. Two toilets and an

extra shower, because, in this country, a shower is considered a necessi-
ty. Americans prefer showers to baths. A negress named Hazel comes in
and cleans up whenever we let the place get too dirty. She is expensive,
like all labour here: eleven shillings for half a day.

Wystan is near here, on the coast, at a place called Laguna, which
looks not unlike the south of France. But I must remind you that archi-
tecture, of any kind of meaning, simply doesn't exist. The most beautiful things are the pump-heads of the oil-wells. At night, if you drive
through them, it is like a great dead forest.

*Journey to a War* has just come out. I hear we are getting good
notices, but haven't seen them, yet.

Love to you both. I think of you very often.

C.


September 5
7136 Silver Bow Drive
Hollywood, Cal.

My darling Mummy,
I was so relieved to get your cable and hear you were safe at
Brabyns.[44] I hope you got my reply?

All through this crisis, I've postponed writing to you—hoping I
could do so after it was all over.[45] And now there seems nothing to say.
You know how I feel about this war.

Viertel and I have been living on the radio, day and night.
Now we must pull ourselves together, somehow, and get on with the
film. That seems the most practical work I can do, right now. Later,
unless I see some other way of being useful here, I shall come to

Europe—perhaps with an American Red Cross unit: I'd like that best, I think.

What will happen to Richard?

Heinz, I suppose, will soon be in Poland. It doesn't bear thinking about.

I will write again soon. Take care of yourself.

> All my love,
> C.

They have changed the name of our street, as above.

September 25
303 South Amalfi Drive
Santa Monica, California

My darling Mummy,

Still no news of you, since your last-minute pre-war letter. Thank God you are at Brabyns. I wrote you there, the day after it started, but only a short note, because I didn't quite know what to say—and I don't now. I can well imagine how ghastly these three weeks have been for you. Here, the war is the one topic of our conversation—especially at Viertel's, where I spend most of the day, working on this film. The news-service is extremely efficient. I expect we know as much about what is happening as anybody—which isn't a great deal. Sentiment here is, of course, strongly pro-Ally; but most people are for staying out at present. If France were being invaded and the Allies beaten, I think feeling would swing round quickly in favour of intervention.

My own feeling you know already. I loathe the whole business, and feel that I ought to be in the middle of it. As a nearly-American citizen, I am not liable to English conscription. If this war goes on, I shall try to join an American Red Cross unit, get some training, and then come over. At present, there is my work here, and I shall try to get on with it. I think this is right. I hope so. What do you feel, yourself?

What is going to happen to Richard? This worries me a lot. Surely, they won't put him in the Army?

Viertel is nearly crazy, though a little better now. We nearly had to chain him down to prevent his going to London, where he would be worse than useless. The house is full of arm-chair generals, whose nerves have gone to pieces and who scream at each other and come near to blows. Meanwhile, outside, the flowers bloom and the Pacific smiles, and everything is utterly unreal and mad. How does one live through such a time? Only by working at one's job, counting to fifty before speaking, and remembering the Hundred Years' War, the Thirty Years' War, the Kaiser, Napoleon, etc etc. It also does no harm to remember Spain, and the extreme equanimity with which most of us bore its sufferings.

We have left our house, and moved into these rooms, which are far more economical and quite as nice. The weather has been very hot indeed, but tonight is much cooler. It's raining. Harvey is going to art school again. I am in good health. But it's no good—I can't talk about anything except the War, so won't depress you with writing any more. At any rate, don't worry about me for the present, because there's nothing to worry about. I think of you continually, darling, and dread what you must be feeling. I would rather you were *quite* safe, at Penmaenmawr, but no doubt Brabyns gives you more to do, and doing is the only distraction.

How about Nanny and Elizabeth?[46] Love to all.

As always,

C.

October 15
303 South Amalfi Drive
Santa Monica, California

My darling Mummy,

I was very glad to get your letter and hear that you are safe in
Wales, and that R. has got satisfactory work.[47] But I do hope you won't
think of going back to London, now that it really seems likely the raids
may begin. Like you, I still feel that there *may* be some quick solution of the whole business—if only because events are developing so
fast. Goodness only knows what changes in the map will have been
made by Christmas! Sentiment here remains strongly pacifist, strongly
pro-Ally, strongly convinced that the U.S.A. will come in, sooner or
later. We are dazed with news—much of which is the new utterly futile
kind of literary reporting: "As I write these lines, a lark is singing high
above Montparnasse (or Golder's Green, or Unter den Linden, or the
Kremlin). It seems difficult to realize . . . etc etc."

It is still very hot—almost too hot to lie on the beach. Day after
day, this marvelous cloudless weather continues. And so does our work
on the film. It is about the career of a Nazi. How it started, how it
developed, how it ended. But there are all manner of difficulties with
the people in New York who are financing it. And, anyhow, it could
hardly be produced until after the Neutrality Act has been in some way
amended or adjusted—if it ever is.

In the intervals, Viertel and I write short stories, plan other films
and read to each other out of the classics. It is necessary to keep oneself
occupied every hour of the day. Otherwise, you just curl up like a dog,
in dumb misery, against the radio. Then I go to see Gerald Heard, and,
for a few hours, everything becomes tolerable and sane. He feels all this
too, but in quite a different way—and in proportion to all other kinds of
suffering everywhere. That is so important. The rest of us here are so apt

to identify this war with ourselves, to make it the special private sorrow of our ego. Indeed, the Emigration have taken complete possession of the war, and are ready to wage it to the last drop of the last English boy's blood—which is infuriating, but quite natural. Viertel, knowing England and having English friends, stands out against this attitude passionately.

Wystan is in New York, and will stay there, it seems, for the present. I wish I could be with him, but there seems little chance of earning a living there, and the atmosphere is far crazier and more jittery in the East. I shan't go back unless there is something definite to do. Harvey Young has started a small pottery business with a friend. They make horrible pseudo-Mexican ware. The best that can be said of it is that, at least, it doesn't explode!

I look at the sea, which is lonely and wet, now that the sun is setting, and I think of you, too, looking at the sea. How long is it since I was in Penmaenmawr? Life seems to have gone by in a moment. How does yours seem to you? I wish we were together and could talk—because now I don't feel that you are any particular age, or that I am any particular age. Or even, especially, that you're my Mother. There's so much I want to ask—so much I should have asked, instead of lecturing you from the sitting-room fireplace—simply as a fellow traveller. I have often made you very unhappy; but, believe me, I have been punished for it—so severely punished that I don't need to apologize. My punishment has been that I have always, in one way or another, made the people I loved behave to me as I behaved to you. Goodness, how long it takes to learn.

Well, no more now. May the ship which carries this letter escape U-boats.

> All my love (and, of course,
> remembrances to Maude)[48]
> C.

November 18
303 South Amalfi Drive
Santa Monica, California

My darling Mummy,

Thank you very much for the three letters, which arrived in a bunch. I am so relieved that you seem to have settled down in Penmaenmawr and are not showing signs of wanting to return permanently to London. Because one never knows when the bombing may start in earnest. Not that I expect it, just yet, in spite of all Hitler's threats.

Richard's job sounds strenuous. None of my friends seem to be doing anything half so nationally important. To drive a cow is surely better than to censor a letter, and several of them are censors, I hear. Stephen is starting a magazine, Beatrix acting with a small group of her own in an unheated theatre for hardly any money. No news of Ian, who might be in the army.[49]

Please don't worry about my state of mind! The moaning of neutrals is of no importance, anyhow; and I have ceased to moan. "The war" is a horror, but so was "the peace" which preceded it ; and "the peace" which follows probably won't be much better. Until people somehow come to their senses, no war and no armistice will make much difference. War will keep moving about the world, like the swarm of locusts in *The Good Earth,* and settling on one place after another. Everybody gets their turn. So one has to keep on with one's job and pray that one's friends won't be hurt, and wait and wait.

I have just started working for Goldwyn, making a spy-film around the character of Mr Norris. There isn't much money in it, but at least I can begin paying my debts and settle up the rent. And it is a beginning, if I do decide to go on working in pictures.

The canyon is beautiful, now that we have a kind of autumn-summer—the loveliest time of the year here. You can still lie on the beach, and the sky is blue without a single cloud. Berthold collaborates with me. So I see him every day. Harvey Young keeps on drawing. It is all very peaceful.

My further movements depend a lot on Wystan. He still hasn't got his quota, and might have to leave altogether. But I don't hear much from New York.

You needn't worry about our minds being poisoned by German propaganda! If there is any, nobody reads it. There is an excellent American broadcast direct from Berlin—extremely critical: I often wonder that the Nazis permit it. But, of course, it can't be heard in Germany, as it is short-wave.

I just received the new number of *New Writing*—the last, till the war is over, apparently. Am rather surprised that he is risking such a large edition of *Goodbye to Berlin*. But maybe people read a lot nowadays. I suppose one ought to devote oneself to keeping everybody amused. Well, I'm doing my bit, with this film. Nothing could be more artificial: it's like an eighteenth century Italian comedy. But it ought to be quite lively.

I will try sending this letter by the clipper. Because I feel sure that at least two of mine have been lost. And you'll get it quicker.

My love to Maude, Nanny, Richard (when you write) and very much to yourself.

C.

November 27
303 South Amalfi Drive
Santa Monica, California

My darling Mummy,

Thank you for your letters. I'm afraid mine seem to be getting lost—I can't imagine why. However, I have sent one off last week by air-mail, and I shall send this one the same way.

Still busy working at Goldwyn's. In fact, I now have my office there, and a secretary, and two telephones. But all this splendour is precarious, like the position of the great nobles in the Elizabethan period. Goldwyn is said to dislike my first treatment of the story extremely, and I am waiting at this moment for what is promised as a highly unpleasant interview with him! However, he can't very well fire me at once, as I am under contract for another three weeks.

The weather is still beautiful, though chilly at nights. Yesterday and the day before, we went for picnics—one to the top of Mount Wilson, where there is an observatory and a magnificent view of the whole valley, right away to the ocean; you can see more than a hundred miles—the other to a big canyon in the mountains. This was a very large picnic, including the Huxleys, Garbo, Bertrand Russell and Krishnamurti—an all-star cast which you would hardly find the equal of in any other place, I should think![50] I am getting to like Huxley rather better. He makes great efforts to be pleasant, but he is so very very donnish. Garbo is very silly and gay and sympathetic. If she weren't Garbo, I could be great friends with her—but she is so terribly isolated: always having to cover her face with her hand or hat when we pass anyone, for fear of being recognized. It is like going around with someone who is wanted for murder. Russell I didn't get a chance of talking to. He seemed a typical English aristocrat eccentric, very amiable and talkative. Krishnamurti was most unassuming: I can understand how much he disliked being a Messiah. I asked him about Leonard.[51] He said oh yes, he'd seen him quite a lot, on and off, and gave me an address where he thought I could reach him. It seems that Leonard is or has been working some kind of Government job, so I imagine he has abandoned the fruit-farm. He is believed to be living right here in Los Angeles. I will try to find out.

Have just been to see Goldwyn. He was much more agreeable than I had expected; but whether I shall ever succeed in pleasing him is another story. I am going back now to consult with Viertel.

No news from Wystan for a long time. Perhaps he has gone to Canada about his quota. I am very glad I am not in New York, where they are all freezing.

My future plans remain as uncertain as the course of the war. It is impossible to know what may have happened by the spring. Most people seem to agree that America could not afford to let the Allies lose; but as long as they aren't losing, and as long as there are no sensational air-raids on open cities in the west of Europe, public opinion is likely to be content with fairly open pro-allied sympathy, and selling munitions. Some quite well-informed people I have talked to seem to feel that, even if the United States were involved, the war-effort from this country should be confined to supplying armaments, and a skeleton army of engineers to work the machines. The disadvantages of participating in a big way are very clearly understood here; and the general opinion is certainly violently opposed to sending American boys to the battlefields. Also, it is felt that, if America actually enters the war, America could play a much less effective part in helping to arbitrate a just peace.

I think of you all a great deal; and hope you are getting through the clammy Welsh winter. Give my love to Richard, Nanny, Maude and the others.

As Always,
C.

December 5
303 So. Amalfi Drive
Santa Monica, California

My darling Mummy,

It is heartbreaking to get these letters from you, all complaining
that I don't write. Quite aside from the previous letters, which I sent
by water, I am now writing for the third consecutive week by air-mail.
Other people seem to get these Clipper letters without fail, and surely
there is nothing in mine which the censor could object to! But no
doubt they'll eventually arrive, all in a bunch.

There isn't very much news. I am still working for Goldwyn, and
still failing to give satisfaction. My spies are either not clever enough, or
not daring enough, or too funny, or too dull. Goldwyn has also taken
a personal dislike to *Mr Norris,* which, naturally, I resent. However, I
work patiently on and on, turning out new versions, and endeavouring
to earn my large salary. I think the job will come to an end two weeks
from now; but there are several others in prospect.

Viertel is very much excited, as Beatrix has at last signified that
she might be willing to come over and act the part of the servant-girl
in New York. Personally, I am afraid that *They Walk Alone* might not
have much success here: the whole setting is too unfamiliar. And the
subject isn't fundamentally interesting enough. New Yorkers like their
serious plays to be problem-plays. She would do far better in something classical: Ibsen, for example. But even if the play is a flop, I think
she's bound to have a personal success, which will lead to something
else later.

I am so delighted that Ethel's book has been chosen by the
Book Society.[52] What a shame that it had to happen now—and not six
months ago! But maybe the war has stimulated reading? We are told it
has. Please *don't* send the book over. I wouldn't know what to do with it,

and it would cost you a lot. Some people tell me that there is difficulty about sending books out of England at all, but I don't believe this, as I received two the other day, from John Lehmann.

This fantastic weather continues. Yesterday and the day before it was still warm enough to go swimming! I believe there is a very unpleasant rainy season later, and lots of ocean fog.

Slowly, I am getting around to the idea of writing again. But it won't be anything like what I have done so far. Philosophical, probably, and deeply religious! Very obscure. Full of visions and dreams. It sounds awful, doesn't it? Perhaps it's only a reaction from movie work.

I expect you are doing a good deal of reading and meditating yourself. Penmaenmawr in winter must make one very introspective. But I thank goodness you are safe, and that R. is securely fitted into the war-work economy. And I still continue to hope that we shall see extraordinary changes before spring. I must repeat, as this seems to bother you, that we are *very* well-informed here, and you needn't picture us living in a fog of rumours and alarms. Of course, nobody knows what Russia is really up to—but then, nobody knows that anywhere, except in the Kremlin.

> All my love, and greetings
> to the others,
> Christopher

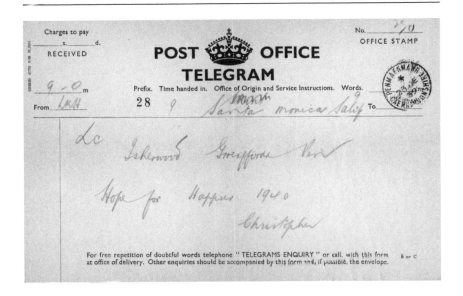

[Telegram from Santa Monica, California]

[December 23]

HOPE FOR HAPPIER 1940

Christopher

# *Editor's Notes*

## 1935

1. Heinz Neddermeyer (often referred to as H.) was Isherwood's German boyfriend. They met in Berlin when Heinz was seventeen, and their relationship quickly became the most serious one of Isherwood's life up until that time.

2. Paul Kryger was a student in Cophenhagen and was apparently a friend of Stephen Spender's.

3. Heinz had attempted to join Isherwood in London in 1934 but was turned away at Harwich by British immigration. He was challenged for being an illegal worker, but the official reason he was denied entry was "moral."

4. Michael Spender, Stephen Spender's older brother, and his German wife, Erica, who were living in Copenhagen at the time. (See note 22 regarding Stephen Spender.)

5. Edward Upward was Isherwood's longtime friend. They met at Repton in 1921 and then both went to Corpus Christi College, Cambridge. The two shared literary interests and Marxist leanings, though Upward was much more dedicated to the Communist ideology than Isherwood. He was a close and trusted friend throughout Isherwood's life.

6. Durrants was a review subscription service.

7. *Mr Norris Changes Trains*, which Isherwood often refers to as *Mr Norris*.

8. Richard Isherwood was Christopher's brother. He was seven years younger than Christopher and had continuous problems in school and in his adulthood. Like Christopher, Richard was homosexual, though Katherine Bucknell suggests that because he lived with Kathleen throughout his adult life and was awkward and shy, he had little

opportunity to develop any long-term relationships (*Diaries,* 958). Christopher gave the Marple estate to him, where he lived reclusively until it was condemned.

9. Olive Mangeot was the English wife of the Belgian violinist André Mangeot. Isherwood worked for a year as a secretary to André's string quartet. Olive was warm, easy, and energetic, and, according to Katherine Bucknell, was an attractive rival to Kathleen in the role of the mother. Isherwood brought all his friends to meet Olive when he was in London (*Diaries,* 971).

10. I have been unable to determine who Miss Balbernie was.

11. Roger Burford was an old Cambridge friend of Isherwood's, an artist and a writer. He married Stella Wilkinson, who was a painter.

12. Hector Wintle was another old friend from Isherwood's school days at Repton.

13. The novelist Hugh Walpole was born in New Zealand but moved to England with his family when he was five. He wrote several popularly acclaimed novels—and spent some time in Hollywood—but worried that his work was "old fashioned."

14. See note 3.

15. Wystan Hugh Auden was an English poet, playwright, librettist, and, as Katherine Bucknell asserts, "arguably the greatest English poet of the [twentieth] century" (923). Auden and Isherwood met as schoolboys in 1915. They were close friends and collaborators throughout their lives, traveling together and eventually immigrating to the United States, where their lives diverged when Isherwood went to California and Auden remained in New York. Despite their geographical distance and the different worldviews of a Californian and a New Yorker, the two remained quite close until Auden's death in 1973.

16. Harold Nicolson was a diplomat, Member of Pariament (1935–45), and writer; his wife, Vita Sackville-West, was a prominent novelist and close friend of Virginia Woolf, co-owner with her husband, Leonard, of the Hogarth Press, Isherwood's publisher. In the early thirties, Nicolson was editor of *Action,* the New Party's magazine. Auden had got to know him and asked him to look into Heinz's records. Later, Nicolson wrote an article in the *Spectator* challenging Isherwood and Auden's decision to remain in America after war was declared.

17. Curtis Brown is a literary agency. Isherwood's agent there was David Higham.

18. Isherwood's uncle, Henry Isherwood. He was Isherwood's father's eldest brother and had inherited Marple Hall and the family estates in Cheshire. He provided Isherwood with an allowance for a time and made him his heir upon his death, but Isherwood passed the inheritance on to Richard.

19. Hector Wintle, see note 12.

20. Isherwood was godfather to Hector's son.

21. Later called *The Dog beneath the Skin*, often referred to as *Dogskin*. Parker writes that it was to be the centerpiece of the Group Theatre's new season at the Westminster Theatre (294). See 1936, note 14.

22. Stephen Spender was an English poet, critic, and editor. He was introduced to Isherwood by Auden, and the three had a close, if vexed, relationship. He and his then boyfriend, Tony Hyndman, shared a house with Isherwood and Heinz in Portugal, during the winter of 1935–36. His marriage to Inez Pearn in 1939 (among other things) distanced him somewhat from Isherwood, but he was very involved in defending Auden's and Isherwood's reputations in England after they came under harsh criticism for their pacifism and move to the United States.

23. Isherwood's uncle Henry, see note 18.

24. A prolific British writer and novelist, Mackenzie served as rector of Glasgow University and as literary critic for the London *Daily Mail*.

25. Gerald Hamilton, whom Isherwood met in Berlin, was the model for Mr Norris. Hamilton was almost pathologically dishonest—and perhaps even criminal—but charming, eccentric, and entertaining, at home at almost every rung of society. He was very involved in Isherwood's attempts to obtain a new nationality for Heinz. Isherwood variously refers to him as Mr Norris, Arthur (the character's first name), or Gerald. I have put "Mr Norris" in italics whenever he is referring to the novel.

26. See note 12.

27. Berthold Viertel was a Viennese writer and film director, whom Isherwood had met in London. He hired Isherwood to work on his film *Little Friend* and later worked with him in Hollywood. Isherwood modeled Friedrich Bermann in *Prater Violet* after Viertel.

28. A sketch of Berlin life that was included in *Goodbye to Berlin*.

29. Gerald Hamilton was famous for exploiting his identity as the "real" Mr. Norris and caused Isherwood some embarrassment on occasion.

30. Isherwood wrote many reviews for the *Listener,* a literary magazine edited by his friend the writer J. R. Ackerley.

31. Klaus Mann was the eldest son of Thomas Mann. Klaus was also a writer, as well as an editor, journalist, and occasional actor. He and Isherwood met in Berlin in the early thirties. Isherwood wrote a memorial essay for Klaus, which was later reprinted in *Exhumations,* after he committed suicide in 1949.

32. This probably refers to Hamilton's autobiography, *As Young as Sophocles,* which Isherwood helped him revise.

33. It seems Isherwood refers here to Gerald Hamilton by his fictional name, Arthur. "I oppose it, but I profit from it."

34. The Monkhouses lived close to the Isherwoods near Marple. Isherwood was an intimate friend of Patrick Monkhouse's during their adolescence. Patrick's father, Allan, wrote a novel in which one of the characters, Marmaduke, is supposed to have been modeled on the young Isherwood. Rachel Monkhouse was in love with Isherwood, whereas he was attracted to the younger brother John. Rachel married and lived at Wyberslegh during the thirties.

35. Isherwood's nanny, Annie Avis, had been with Kathleen since Isherwood's early childhood. Paul Kryger, see note 2.

36. Mr. Symonds was the family solicitor.

37. Wyberslegh Hall. The fifteenth-century manor house where Isherwood was born and where Kathleen and Richard lived after World War II. It was part of the Bradshaw Isherwood estate.

38. Isherwood gives a copy of the play each to the unknown Miss Balbernie, Gerald Hamilton, Olive Mangeot, and Berthold Viertel.

39. Humphrey Spender was Stephen Spender's younger brother and a friend of Isherwood's. He was an avid photographer and took many pictures of Isherwood and his circle in Berlin and later in Portugal.

40. This is the character sketch "The Turn Round the World," based on two passengers Isherwood and Heinz met on a ferry during their trip to the Canary Islands in 1934.

41. *Paul is Alone,* a work he later abandoned.

42. John Lehmann met Isherwood in the early thirties when he worked at the Hogarth Press. Lehmann convinced Leonard and Virginia Woolf to publish *The Memorial* after it had been rejected by Jonathan Cape. Lehmann published most of the short pieces that would later be the complete *Goodbye to Berlin* in his newly founded journal, *New Writing.*

43. William Robson-Scott met Isherwood in 1932 in Berlin, where he was lecturing at Berlin University. Katherine Bucknell mentions that he summered at Ruegen Island with Isherwood, Heinz Neddermeyer, Stephen Spender, and others, and was a close friend to Isherwood during the 1930s (988). Isherwood dedicated *Lions and Shadows* to him.

44. Isherwood was thinking of moving with Heinz to South Africa in order to pursue a new nationality for him.

45. Rudolph Katz was an economist and dedicated Marxist when Isherwood met him in Berlin in the early thirties. He left Germany in 1933, finally settling in Argentina, where he became director of the journal *Economic Survey*.

46. The high-strung Richard did not like to travel and often became very upset when faced with unfamiliar places.

47. "The Turn Round the World," see note 40.

48. An English painter and friend of Isherwood's in London during the twenties. He died, as Isherwood relates, in a freak accident in his studio in St. Tropez, France.

49. See note 12.

50. David Higham was Isherwood's agent at Curtis Brown.

51. Geoffrey Bles was a London-based publisher of C. S. Lewis, Jacques Maritain, and other well-regarded writers.

52. Apparently, Uncle Henry was making plans to accompany Kathleen on her visit to Amsterdam.

53. Graham Greene, an English writer who converted to Catholicism, was also Isherwood's cousin. Whether adventure thrillers, complex psychological studies, or essays, Greene's work always reflects a struggle with moral and spiritual dilemmas.

54. E. M. Forster was an English novelist and essayist often associated with the Bloomsbury group. As Bucknell mentions, Forster was a literary hero for Isherwood, who directed the publication of Forster's homosexual-themed novel *Maurice* after Forster's death in 1970 (941). He was always a supporter of Isherwood, even when public sympathy turned against him during the war.

55. Anton (Toni) Altmann, the Bavarian boyfriend of Brian Howard (no doubt the friend mentioned here). Sometimes Isherwood spells his name "Tony."

56. Brian Howard was an English poet (of American parentage) and, as Katherine Bucknell describes, an aesthete (953). Known primarily for being "exceedingly dissolute," he was the model for Anthony Blanche in Evelyn Waugh's *Brideshead Revisited* and Ambrose Silk in Waugh's *Put Out More Flags,* and never really lived up to his potential as a writer. Like Isherwood and Heinz, Howard and Altmann were turned away by British immigration officals, and Howard moved to various cities in Europe trying to find a place to live with Toni.

57. Bob Buckingham was a policeman and longtime friend of Forster's.

58. In attendance at this impromptu birthday party were E. M. Forster, Bob Buckingham, Stephen Spender, Gerald Hamilton, Klaus Mann, Brian Howard, and Toni Altmann.

59. Fräulein Thurau was Isherwood's landlady in Berlin. She and her eccentric tenants were inspiration for material in several of the Berlin stories.

60. It is not certain to whom this refers.

61. Isherwood and Heinz are leaving for Portugal.

62. Miss Mitchell was their English landlady.

63. Stephen Spender and his then companion, Tony Hyndman, were living with Isherwood and Heinz in Portugal.

64. Elizabeth was Kathleen's longtime cook.

## 1936

1. Colonel Alexander Kearsey was one of Frank Ishwerwood's fellow officers during his service in South Africa and one of Isherwood's godfathers.

2. Probably *Paul is Alone.*

3. This sketch was published as "The Nowaks."

4. *The Dog beneath the Skin* opened at the Westminster Theatre in London on January 30, 1936, according to Parker (314). This is a bit confusing because the letter suggests that Kathleen had seen it already. She may have attended one of the rehearsals, which took place in December 1935, or she may be referring to a review of the published play, released by Faber and Faber in May 1935.

5. Olive Mangeot, see 1935, note 9.

6. Miss Mitchell was their English landlady.

7. Lady Carrick ruled over the English colony in Portugal.

8. Humphrey Spender, see 1935, note 39.

9. Allan Monkhouse, see 1935, note 34.

10. Forster had surgery for a prostate problem, which was a risky procedure at the time.

11. Edward Upward, see 1935, note 5. Isherwood refers to the first section of his work *Journey to the Border.*

12. At this time Isherwood was writing *The Lost.* He says in the introduction to the *Berlin Stories* that he envisioned transforming his Berlin experiences "into one huge tightly constructed melodramatic novel, in the manner of Balzac," which is perhaps why he requested that his mother send him copies of Balzac's novels.

13. Isherwood's uncle John (Jack) Isherwood.

14. Rupert Doone was an English dancer, choreographer, and theatrical producer and founder of the Group Theatre, the cooperative for which Auden and Isherwood wrote plays in the thirties.

15. King George V died on January 20, 1936, and lay in state in Westminster Hall. Graham Greene wrote a patriotic article at the occasion in which he comments on the closeness that the ordinary people felt for the king and suggests that any past wrongs are now forgiven: "Their silence and grief are his acquittal."

16. Gerald Hamilton, see 1935, note 25.

17. Anton Altmann, also known as "Toni," see 1935, note 55. The party of seven consisted of Isherwood and Heinz, Stephen Spender and Tony Hyndman, Gerald Hamilton, Brian Howard, and Toni Altmann.

18. See 1935, note 32.

19. There is a discrepancy here: a handwritten note on the original of this letter states that this money is for English performing rights, which is confusing because in the following letter, Isherwood asserts that the money is *not* for English performing rights.

20. It seems the novel *The Last of Mr. Norris* appeared erroneously in the American catalog under the title *The Luck and the Ell*.

21. Isherwood's uncle Henry Isherwood, see 1935, note 18.

22. This reference is uncertain.

23. Mrs. Lanigan was the mother of a boy Isherwood tutored during the summer of 1929. According to Parker, the job was "not very taxing and ended with Isherwood's dismissal," but was significant because Isherwood had with Mrs. Lanigan his "first—and last—complete sex experience with a woman" (177).

24. E. M. Forster.

25. In an interview, Forster explained that the piece in question quoted from a pamphlet in which one Nile engineer attacked (in print) another over some technical matter and was sued in Egypt. The plaintiff won, so the republication of the piece in *Arbinger Harvest* became libelous.

26. It is difficult to know who this refers to other than to one of the eccentric exiles living in Portugal at the time.

27. Mrs. Mitchell was the mother of Miss Mitchell, Isherwood's landlady.

28. Fräulein Schroeder is the landlady in the *Berlin Stories*. The character is based on Isherwood's Berlin landlady, Fräulein Thurau.

29. These sketches later became *Goodbye to Berlin.*

30. Isherwood abandoned his work on *Paul is Alone.*

31. Isherwood tutored Ian Scott-Kilvert in the twenties and planned to write an autobiographical sketch of this time called "In the Day Nursery." Isherwood was apparently quite taken with some essays the eight-year-old Scott-Kilvert had written for his governess and stole the boy's notebook.

32. Robert Moody was a friend and fellow student from medical school, who had been at Oxford with Auden.

33. Later, in 1941, one of Isherwood's jobs at MGM was to write a prologue for the British film adaptation of this book. It is about a miner's son who wants to become an MP.

34. Marjorie Ross was a friend of Kathleen's. Isherwood tutored her son in 1927.

35. Basil Fry was a cousin of Kathleen's. Isherwood visited him in Germany in 1928, when Fry was the British vice-consul in Bremen.

36. Robson-Scott's friend was Rico Bixener.

37. Mrs. Loweth was a neighbor in Sintra who also kept chickens.

38. Apparently, Heinz is staying with Mrs. Loweth because he had been called up for his military duties by the German authorities, and Isherwood believed it was better that he stay at an address other than the one known to the German consulate. Although Isherwood says here that Heinz stayed with Mrs. Loweth, Peter Parker writes that Heinz also stayed with an English family called Norton, but that they had asked him to leave, fearing his presence would jeopardize their own standing in the country (324).

39. James Stern was the same age as Isherwood and was also a writer with a rather aristocratic upbringing. Tania Stern was a physical therapist who later offered to train Heinz as a masseur. The Sterns moved into the villa with Isherwood and Heinz.

40. Stern knew Cyril Connolly and Brian Howard at Eaton.

41. Salinger was an English lawyer in Brussels whom Gerald Hamilton had enlisted to help obtain naturalization papers for Heinz. Isherwood asked his mother for the rather large sum of £1,000, which he would then pass on to Salinger through Hamilton. Kathleen was very suspicious about both of these men and their intentions.

42. Robert Moody, see note 32.

43. The Mexican official seems to have been the chargé d'affaires at the Mexican legation in Brussels.

44. Stella and Roger Burford were old friends who assumed the lease of the house in Sintra and had agreed to take Isherwood's papers back to England when he left for Belgium. See 1935, note 11.

45. G. B. Smith was Isherwood's history tutor at Repton.

46. The bridge of Heinz's nose had been broken in a childhood fight, and increasingly he had trouble breathing. He was advised to have a tonsillectomy and to have the bridge reconstructed to correct the problem.

47. Edward Upward had recently married Hilda Percival.

48. Probably Stephen Spender's book *The Destructive Element*.

49. Robert Moody, see note 32.

50. Jean Ross, the model for Sally Bowles.

51. This reference is to *Lions and Shadows*.

52. G. B. Smith, Isherwood's history tutor, Edward Upward, Hector Wintle, his work for André Mangeot's string quartet, Bill de Lichtenberg, W. H. Auden, an old friend called Maunder, and Robert Moody.

53. Mrs. Norton wrote children's books. Parker writes that Heinz stayed with her family for a couple of days in Portugal in an attempt to dodge the authorities, but the arrangement did not work out. See note 38.

54. Spender had recently married Inez Pearn.

55. "The Turn Round the World," originally published in the *Listener,* was included in *The Best British Short Stories 1936,* edited by Edward J. O'Brien for Houghton Mifflin.

56. This suggests that O'Brien might have wanted to include Auden's story in the collection as well, but there isn't any record of its being anthologized anywhere. Also Isherwood wanted it for research for *Lions and Shadows*.

57. King Edward VIII was said to have Nazi sympathies. He abdicated the throne in December 1936 in order to marry the American divorcée Wallis Simpson.

58. Isherwood's uncle Jack, Colonel Alexander Kearsey, and Rachel Monkhouse.

59. Tony Hyndman, see 1935, note 63. Giles Romilly was a nephew of Winston Churchill. He and his brother Esmond created a scandal when they published, as schoolboys at Wellington College, a left-wing, antiestablishment magazine called *Out of Bounds*. Giles had written a notorious piece about homosexual activity at the school; the article was banned.

# 1937

1. Robert Hale, the publisher of Brecht's work under the title *A Penny for the Poor*.

2. Auden was on his way to Spain to help the Republican cause against the Fascists in the Spanish civil war.

3. After Spender married Inez Pearn, his lover Tony Hyndman joined the International

Brigade and went to fight in the Spanish civil war. Although he had become a communist, he grew disillusioned in Spain and became a pacifist. He deserted and was imprisoned; Spender, who also had gone to Spain, helped obtain his release.

4. The papers had printed that Auden was off to fight against the Fascists, but in the letter that Isherwood mentions to Kathleen here, Auden expressed hope that he would be driving an ambulance:

> Dear Christopher,
>
> Herewith *Railway Accident*. I've also asked Edward to send you the Byron [?] letter which he has.
>
> I'm going to Spain in early January either Ambulance driving or fighting. I hope the former. Is there any chance of seeing you in Paris on my way through. In case of accident remember that you and Edward are executors. I'm asking Faber in the event of my getting killed to pay out £100 at once to go to Michael to help with his final education. After that all cash is yours . . . I enclose a suggested contract from the G.T. [Group Theatre] What do you think? Ashley Dukes wants it to go on at the Duchess after Murder in the Cathedral. Better than the Westminster I think.  Best love and Xmas greetings, Wystan.

5. James and Tania Stern, see 1936, note 39.

6. Brian Howard and Tony Altmann, see 1935, notes 55 and 56.

7. Salinger was in London investigating the possibility of a temporary move back to England.

8. This refers to the 1934 refusal of immigration officers to allow Heinz into England. See 1935, note 3.

9. As a result of Edward VIII's abdication, his brother George was about to be crowned as George VI.

10. Spender was in Spain with the Republicans at the time.

11. Olive Mangeot was deeply suspicious of Gerald Hamilton and thought him both dangerous and criminal.

12. This refers to the incident in which Heinz was in a café that was raided. Peter Parker explains that a woman claimed her necklace had been stolen, so everyone was detained for questioning, at which point it was discovered that Heinz had no identity card. On making further inquiries at the hotel where Heinz was staying, the police were informed that he was a male prostitute. His permission to stay in France was there-

fore revoked, as was his residency permit for Belgium, so Salinger suggested he go to Luxembourg.

13. There are no letters to Kathleen between May 5 and August 17, and it was during this time that Heinz was arrested by the Gestapo—after he was expelled from Luxembourg—tried and sentenced to six months in prison, one year of labor service, and two years of military service. Isherwood was in Brussels at the time of Heinz's arrest and returned to London after the trial in the middle of June, moving into his old room at Pembroke Gardens (so he wouldn't have needed to write to Kathleen). Parker writes that Isherwood made very few diary entries that summer and suggests that Isherwood dealt with his grief by taking several lovers and getting a lot of work done (350–54). At the end of August, he and Auden go to Dover.

14. Isherwood and Auden are working on *On the Frontier*.

15. Presumably, Sylvain Mangeot, son of André and Olive.

## 1938

1. This is the beginning of Isherwood and Auden's trip to China to write the travel book *Journey to a War*.

2. Rupert Doone, who was planning to direct *On the Frontier* with the Group Theatre. See also 1936, note 14.

3. Hugh Chisholm was a young American with whom Isherwood had a brief relationship during the summer of 1937. He had wanted to join Isherwood and Auden for part of their trip to China, but they decided he was too young.

4. Ian Scott-Kilvert was Isherwood's former pupil (see 1936, note 31). He hadn't seen Scott-Kilvert in almost ten years when they became reacquainted before he and Auden left for China. Isherwood had become quite smitten with Scott-Kilvert and had visited him in Cambridge, where he was attending Caius College. Heinz and Isherwood corresponded occasionally after Heinz's release from prison in November 1937. He lived in Berlin with his aunt before he began his labor service.

5. Peter Fleming was a well-known travel writer who was sent to China by the *Times*. Isherwood and Auden accompanied Fleming on a tour of the southeastern front.

6. To assuage the guilt he felt about Heinz's arrest, Isherwood sent him money and presents, although he worried about getting him into trouble with the Gestapo. In 1938, Heinz began his labor service on a building site at the Potsdamer Platz; he then had to fulfill two years of military service. Whether Isherwood planned to reconnect with Heinz

after he had done his military service is questionable, and it became moot after Isherwood moved to the United States and war broke out. Heinz ended the war in an American prisoner of war camp in France. He returned to Germany, married, and had a son. Isherwood saw him again—and met his wife—during a visit to Berlin in 1952.

7. Evelyn Waugh, the novelist and critic. The reviews Isherwood refers to here are probably of *Lions and Shadows,* which was published by Hogarth on March 17. Waugh admired Isherwood's style and wit, but he judged both Isherwood and Auden harshly for their political views. After it was published by Faber, *Journey to a War* was reviewed by Waugh in the *Spectator* on March 24, 1939.

8. German troops entered Austria in March, and Hitler declared the two countries unified.

9. Tony Hyndman, see 1935, note 22; 1937, note 3. Isherwood spent a fair amount of time with him after Spender married. Gerald Hamilton was living in Brussels at the time.

10. Isherwood and Auden were both in Brussels to finish *Journey to a War,* while Isherwood was also correcting proofs for *Goodbye to Berlin.*

11. Jacky Hewit was the son of a riveter, former dancer, and the recent lover of Guy Burgess. Hewit hoped to accompany Isherwood to the United States, which never happened, but he did stay with him in Brussels.

12. Cuthbert Worsley was a journalist and one of Tony Hyndman's lovers after Spender married Inez Pearn.

# 1939

1. Thomas Mann was a German novelist and essayist who was awarded the Nobel Prize in 1929. Mann and his family, which included Erika and Klaus, were vocal critics of the Nazi regime and left Germany in 1933. Auden had married his daughter Erika (see note 2, below). Mann was a visiting professor at Princeton, where Isherwood met him, and then moved his family to Pacific Palisades in Southern California, joining a growing European exile community.

2. Auden had married Erika Mann in 1935, after Isherwood had declined. She was about to have her German citizenship revoked, making it impossible for her to leave the country or travel abroad. Her marriage to Auden automatically made her a British subject and therefore able to leave Germany. She moved to the United States, and the *Daily Express* reported that Auden's move there would enable him "to be reunited with his wife" and reported the circumstances of their marriage. The article contained details that could

only have come from someone who knew Auden personally. Peter Parker suggests that the source was most likely Gerald Hamilton (420).

3. It is not certain to whom or to what this refers.

4. Jacky Hewit, see 1938, note 11.

5. Chris Wood was the talented, wealthy, handsome partner of Gerald Heard, and secretly funded many of Heard's projects (Bucknell 1012). He and Heard moved to Los Angeles in 1937.

6. Kathleen must have felt some vindication that Salinger was finally exposed. It is not certain who Dr. Imiantoff is, or what his connection was to Salinger.

7. Colonel Alexander Kearsey, see 1936, note 1.

8. This is probably "Hewit." The text is a bit difficult to read.

9. Lincoln Kirstein was an American impresario in dance and theater, an author, editor, and philanthropist. He was from a wealthy Boston family and educated at Harvard. He brought George Balanchine to New York, and together they founded the School of American Ballet and the New York City Ballet. Kirstein was instrumental in founding the Museum of Modern Art in New York and in defining and promoting the arts in twentieth-century America.

10. E. M. Forster and Stephen Spender.

11. Heinz apparently had injured himself while doing his year of labor service. Isherwood had arranged to send him an allowance during this time. See 1938, note 6.

12. Louis MacNeice was an Anglo-Irish poet who was born in Belfast. He was at Oxford with Auden and Spender and collaborated with Auden on *Letter from Iceland*. He was a prolific writer, a university lecturer, and writer and producer for the BBC.

13. Richard was teaching himself to type. If he should have to go into the army, it was hoped he could land a desk job.

14. Erika Mann.

15. Penmaenmawr was a small seaside town in Colwyn Bay, North Wales, where Isherwood often spent summer holidays with his family during his youth.

16. Harvey Young was a young American who accompanied Isherwood across the country. He is usually referred to as Vernon Old in most of Isherwood's other writings.

17. Ford Maddox Ford, writer, editor, and author of *The Good Soldier* and the tetralogy *Parade's End*. He died in Deauville, France, in 1939, not long after this meeting.

18. Gerald Heard was an Anglo-Irish writer and philosopher. Auden introduced Isherwood to Heard in 1932 when he already had a reputation as commentator for the

BBC and for several books on the evolution of human consciousness. He was friends with Aldous Huxley and other intellectuals of the time, and emigrated to America with Chris Wood and the Huxleys in 1937. He became interested in Eastern religion, yoga, and communal living. He was very influential in Isherwood's life in California, and the two were close friends.

19. Berthold Viertel was a Viennese filmmaker (see 1935, note 27) who had immigrated to Southern California. His descriptions of Hollywood and promise of work were a great lure for Isherwood, and upon his arrival, Isherwood and Viertel renewed their friendship and began working together on a film vaguely inspired by *Mr Norris Changes Trains*.

20. Isherwood met Greta Garbo at the Viertels'.

21. Aldous Huxley was an English novelist and essayist. Isherwood met him through Gerald Heard, and they became close because of their shared interest in pacifism and Eastern religion. Almost blind since his adolescence, Huxley had begun a course of eye exercises based on the Bates Method, which seemed initially to improve his vision.

22. Isherwood is here referring to his paternal uncle Jack. Peter Parker writes that John Isherwood, before marrying, practiced Yoga and embraced fad diets (42).

23. Isherwood's paternal uncle Henry, see 1935, note 18.

24. Many reviewers commented that Auden and Isherwood were callous in their book, *A Journey to a War*. The *Daily Worker* accused them of having "fallen victim to bourgeois subjectivity" and "being too preoccupied with their own psychological plight to be anything but helplessly lost in the struggle of modern China" (Parker 409).

25. He is referring to the September 1938 agreement between England, France, Germany, and Italy that Prime Minister Neville Chamberlain assured Parliament would guarantee "Peace in our time," but which really just gave Hitler part of Czechoslovakia.

26. Isherwood's paternal uncle.

27. Cyril Scott was a composer and his uncle Jack's closest friend as a young man. They shared a flat in London until Jack married.

28. Ludwig Berger was a German film director. Isherwood had worked on a film with him in London, which was based on a story by Carl Zuchmayer, directed by Berger and produced by Alexander Korda.

29. Richard failed his Red Cross examination.

30. Isherwood is referring to his abandonment of medical school.

31. Basil Fry was Kathleen's cousin and the vice-consul in Bremen in the twenties. See 1936, note 35.

32. The British actor Charles Laughton.

33. This refers to an article that suggested that Isherwood and Auden found New York intellectual society "unintelligent, told it so, and donning their shabbiest clothes, shut themselves up in a flat in one of the city's less fashionable slum districts. Here, in conclave, they proceeded to evolve a new philosophy of life . . . Meanwhile the pair have separated. Mr Isherwood has gone off to visit the film stars in Hollywood. Mr Auden is teaching in a boys' school in New England" (Parker 457).

34. Rachel Monkhouse. She lived at Wyberslegh during the thirties. See 1935, note 34.

35. Guy Burgess was a British diplomat and double agent. He became a Communist at Cambridge and was secretly recruited by the Soviets during the thirties. He defected to the USSR in 1951. Isherwood knew Burgess in London, when he, Auden, and Spender were all friends. Burgess and Hewit were lovers until Burgess met Peter Pollock. Burgess introduced Hewit to Isherwood—and the two were lovers for a time—but Burgess lived with Hewit again in the years leading up to his defection (Bucknell 931). Isherwood always felt a bit guilty about his treatment of Hewit. He told Hewit that he would take him to America but then reneged on the offer.

36. Anthony Blunt was an English art historian, Soviet spy, and double agent. Like Burgess, he became a Communist while at Cambridge and was recruited by the Soviets. During his years as a double agent he was named director of the Courtauld Institute of Art and in 1945 became Surveyor of the King's Pictures and continued as Surveyor of the Queen's Pictures under Elizabeth II, who knighted him for his service. He was outed under Margaret Thatcher.

37. Beatrix Lehmann, one of John Lehmann's sisters. She was an actress, and she and Viertel had an affair in 1934.

38. John van Druten was an English playwright who had popular success in both England and America. Both he and Isherwood were pacifists, and he, too, became a U.S. citizen. His strength was light comedy, but he adapted *I Am a Camera,* based on Isherwood's *Goodbye to Berlin.*

39. This is a reference to Chaplin's film *The Great Dictator.*

40. See 1939, note 22.

41. Johnny Weissmuller was the Olympic gold medal swimmer who became the most popular of the screen versions of Tarzan.

42. Swami Prabhavananda was a Hindu monk and founder of the Vedanta Society. Gerald Heard had been studying with him, and Isherwood began to take instruction from him on meditation almost immediately. In 1940 he initiated Isherwood and gave him a

mantra and a rosary. Isherwood lived at the monastery on Ivar Avenue in Hollywood for a while, but he eventually decided that he could not become the monk the swami wished him to be.

43. Thea Mitchell (also known as Miss Mitchell) was Isherwood's eccentric English landlady in Portugal.

44. Brabyns Hall, Cheshire, was near Marple. Kathleen and Richard were staying with friends there.

45. This is the first letter Isherwood wrote to Kathleen after England declared war on Germany on September 3, 1939.

46. Parker writes that Nanny went to stay with her sister in Bury St. Edmonds, and Kathleen's cook, Elizabeth, stayed in London (447).

47. Being unfit for service and having failed his Red Cross exam, Richard performed agricultural service on the farm at Wyberslegh.

48. Maude Brunton (Isherwood left off the *e*) was Kathleen's cousin. Kathleen stayed with her at Penmaenmawr—joined by Nanny—for most of the war.

49. Stephen Spender, who was in London; Beatrix Lehmann, Viertel's lover; and Ian Scott-Kilvert, Isherwood's former pupil and, later, friend.

50. Aldous and Maria Huxley, Greta Garbo, Bertrand Russell, the English philosopher, and Krishnamurti, a Hindu spiritual leader.

51. Possibly Leonard Tristram, the son of an old friend of Kathleen's.

52. Possibly Ethel Colburn Mayne, an old friend of the Isherwoods.

# Index

*Abinger Harvest* (Forster), 56, 64

Ackerley, Joseph Randolph, 18, 20, 25, 29

Alcott, Louisa May, 21, 23, 24, 26

*All the Conspirators* (C. I.), 84, 132, 139, 143

Altmann, Anton (Toni), xiv, 31–32, 33, 51, 167n

Archbishop of Canterbury, 140

*Ascent of F6, The* (C. I. with Auden), 43, 59, 61–62, 63, 80, 87, 134, 143

Auden, Wystan Hugh: in 1938, xiv; in 1939, xv; angry at newspaper coverage, 124; back in New York, 154, 156, 158, 164n, 165n; in Brussels, 117, 118; changes end of *F6*, 143; China trip, 88, 116; collaborating with C. I., 9, 22, 23, 24, 28, 43, 48, 49, 58, 59, 61, 116; film work, 31; gives *Dogskin* to Doone, 50; hates food in New York, 127; help with Heinz, 8; letter to C. I., 172n; likes Harvey Young, 140; in *Lions and Shadows,* 81; meets C. I. in Paris, 87, 90–92; notes to Kathleen, 100, 101, 103; plans to go to Spain, 83; "A Railway Accident," 83; royalties, 131; sails to New York with C. I., 121; sees Doone, 63; takes *F6* to London, 61–62; teaching in United States, 128, 129, 133, 136; as thirties writer, xi; visits Laguna, 150; visits Taos, 138

Avis, Annie (C. I.'s nanny), 166n

Bachardy, Don, xviii

Balbernie, Miss, 6, 22

Balzac, Honoré de, 50; *Illusions Perdues,* 49; *Splendeurs et Misères de Courtisanes,* 49; *Un Grand Homme de Province à Paris,* 49

Baudelaire, Charles: C. I.'s translation of *Journals,* 32

Beethoven, Ludwig von, 24, 48

*Beggar's Opera, The,* 89

Berger, Ludwig, 141

"Berlin Diary" (C. I.), 3, 12, 79

*Best British Short Stories 1936,* 82

Bixner, Rico, 83

Bles, Geoffrey, 29, 167n

Blunt, Anthony, 145, 177n

Brabyns Hall, 178n

Brecht, Bertolt, xiv, 87; C. I.'s translations for *Dreigroschenoper*, 89–90

British Broadcasting Company (BBC), 7

Brunton, Maude, 178n

Buckingham, Bob, 34, 93, 168n

Bucknell, Katherine, x, xiii, xvi

Buonaparte, Miss, 138

Burford, Roger, xiv, 7, 73, 164n, 170n

Burford, Stella, xiv, 7, 73, 164n, 170n

Burgess, Guy, 145, 177n

Byron, George Gordon, Lord: *Childe Harold,* 39

Callam, Mr., 124

Cape. *See* Jonathon Cape (publisher)

Carrick, Ikerrin, 68

Carrick, Lady, 48, 68, 168n

Chamberlain, Neville, xv, 140, 145

Chaplin, Charlie, 147

Chapman & Hall (publisher), 23, 30

Chapter, Sonia, 131

Chisholm, Hugh, 105, 173n

*Christopher and His Kind* (C. I.), viii, ix–x, xvi

Clark Kerr, Sir Archibald, 114

*Club de Femmes* (film), 79

Connolly, Cyril, 132, 144

*Criterion,* 28

*Croquet Player, The* (H. G. Wells), 83

Curtis Brown, Spencer, 52, 56

Curtis Brown (agency), 9, 23, 28, 32, 36, 51, 52, 55, 56, 61, 66, 78, 105, 108, 112, 114, 117, 131, 164n

*Daily Express,* 124

*Daily Mail,* 50, 77, 91

*Daily Telegraph,* 9, 11

*Diaries* (C. I.), xiii

Daladier, Edouard, xv

"Day, The" (C. I.), 67

de la Mare, Mr., 132

de Lichtenberg, Bill, 27, 77, 81, 167n

de Monfreid, Henry: *Hashish,* 20, 26

*Devon Holiday* (Williamson), 28

Dickens, Charles, 11

*Dog Beneath the Skin, The* (C. I. with Auden), 3, 21, 22, 24, 28, 32, 43, 47, 48, 50, 52, 54, 55, 56–58, 59, 78,123

Doone, Rupert, 50, 63, 103, 104–5, 169n

Edward VIII (king), 43, 57, 84

Eliot, T. S.: *Murder in the Cathedral,* 21, 23, 24

*England Have My Bones* (T. H. White), 62

*England Made Me* (Greene), 29

Elizabeth (Kathleen's cook), 168n

"Evening at the Bay" (C. I.), 65–66

*Evening Standard,* 143

Faber and Faber (publisher), 3, 7, 57, 121, 129, 132

*Five Irish Plays* (O'Casey), 51, 56

Fleming, Peter, 106, 108, 113, 114, 173n

Ford, Ford Maddox, 135, 175n

Forster, E. M., xiv, 167n; *Abinger Harvest,*

56, 64; on Elizabeth Bowen, 36; C. I.
doesn't hear from him, 129; libel suit,
64; operation, 48, 60; possible visit
to C. I. in Portugal, 63; visits C. I. in
Amsterdam, 31, 32, 34; visits C. I. in
Brussels, 93; visits C. I. in Portugal,
72; vouches for Heinz's character, 92
Franco, Francisco, 43, 78
Fry, Basil, 69, 142, 170n

Galsworthy, John, 46
Garbo, Greta, 137, 157
Gaumont British, 12, 19, 21
George V (king), xiv, 43, 169n
George VI (king), 43
Goldring, Douglas: *Odd Man Out,* 26
Goldwyn, Samuel, 155, 157, 158, 159
*Goodbye to Berlin* (C. I.), 43, 87, 121, 127,
129, 131, 156
*Good Earth, The* (Pearl S. Buck), 155
Greene, Graham, xiv, 29, 50–51, 78, 167n
Group Theatre, 104, 112, 165n
*Guardian, The,* 113

Hale, Robert, 89, 171n
Hamilton, Gerald, xiv, 34, 35, 51, 74, 83,
95, 116, 118, 125, 165n; collaborates
with C. I. on his autobiography, 25,
53; referred to as Arthur, 19, 21, 25,
31; referred to as Mr. Norris, 11, 14,
29, 30, 32, 94
*Harper's Bazaar,* 108, 112, 117
Harwich incident, 6, 8, 34, 92
*Hashish* (de Monfreid), 20, 26

Hazel (C. I.'s maid in California), 150
Heard, Gerald, 136, 137–38, 140, 149,
175n
*Heartless Land, The* (Stern), 70
Heinemann (publisher), 23, 30
Heinz. *See* Neddermeyer, Heinz
Hewit, Jacky, 118, 125, 126, 145, 146,
174n
Higham, David, 28, 32, 164n, 167n
Hilter, Adolph, xiii, xv, 3, 8, 10, 58, 81,
97, 121, 130, 133, 140, 148
Hogarth Press, 3, 6, 14, 27–28, 30, 34, 60,
97, 121
Howard, Brian, xiv, 33, 39, 77, 167n
*Hunchback of Notre Dame, The* (film), 143
Huxley, Aldous, 137, 147, 157, 176n
Huxley, Maria, 157
Hyndman, Tony, xiv, 3, 39, 40, 43, 53, 83,
85, 116, 165n

Imianitoff, Dr., 125
*In Search of History,* 31
Isherwood, Christopher, works of: *All the
Conspirators,* 84, 132, 139, 143; *The
Ascent of F6* (with Auden), 43, 59,
61–62, 63, 80, 87, 134, 143; "Berlin
Diary," 3, 12, 79; *Christopher and His
Kind,* viii, ix–x, xvi; "The Day," 67;
*Diaries,* xiii; *The Dog beneath the Skin*
(with Auden), 3, 21, 22, 24, 28, 32,
43, 47, 48, 50, 52, 54, 55, 56–58,
59, 78, 123; *Dreigroschenoper* transla-
tion, 89–90; "Evening at the Bay,"
65–66; *Goodbye to Berlin,* 43, 87, 121,

127, 129, 131, 156; *Journey to a War* (with Auden), xv, 97, 121, 127, 129, 132, 150; *Kathleen and Frank: The Autobiography of a Family,* vii–viii; "The Kulaks" (later "The Nowaks"), 46; "The Landauers," 12; *The Last of Mr. Norris* (U.S. edition of *Mr Norris Changes Trains*), 3, 45; *Lions and Shadows,* 43, 87, 97, 108; *The Lost* (later *Goodbye to Berlin*), 65, 66, 105; *The Memorial,* 9, 11, 30, 31; *Mr Norris Changes Trains,* viii, xi, 3, 6, 9, 11, 14, 13, 25, 27, 31, 32, 45, 52, 64, 68, 131, 159; *The North West Passage* (later *Lions and Shadows*), 81; "The Nowaks," 3, 65–66; *On the Frontier* (with Auden), xiv, 87, 104, 126, 131; *Paul is Alone* (abandoned), 3, 43, 52, 57, 65; "Sally Bowles," 43, 79, 87, 106, 108; *A Single Man,* xvi; "The Turn Round the World," 34; *Where is Francis?* (later *The Dog beneath the Skin*) (with Auden), 9–10, 11; "The Winter Term," 67

Isherwood, Henry (uncle), xvi, 9, 11, 12, 21, 29, 60, 67, 89, 138, 164n

Isherwood, John (Jack) (uncle), 50; interest in yoga, 140, 148

Isherwood, Kathleen, vi–viii, viii–ix, xiv; C. I. worries about, 121, 130, 133, 144, 150, 154; passes Red Cross exam, 141, 160; visits C. I. in Amsterdam, 32; visits C. I. in Portugal, 69

Isherwood, Richard, xv, xvi, 6, 26, 30, 63, 163n; C. I. worries about, 121, 130, 152, 160; fails Red Cross exam, 141;

learns to type, 133, 135, 136, 146; war work at Wyberslegh, 153, 155

*It's a Battlefield* (Greene), 29, 50

*Jack and the Ell, The (The Last of Mr. Norris)* (C. I.), 45, 55

James, Henry, 47

*Jenny* (film), 79

Jonathan Cape (publisher), 7, 23, 30, 32; Traveller's Library, 132

*Journey's End,* 59

*Journey to a War* (C. I. with Auden), xv, 97, 121, 127, 129, 132, 150

*Kathleen and Frank: The Autobiography of a Family* (C. I.), vii–viii

Katz, Rudolph, 25, 34, 167n

Kearsey, Colonel Alexander, 45, 126, 168n

Kirstein, Lincoln, 127, 175n

Korda, Alexander, 88

Krishnamurti, 157

Kromer, Tom: *Waiting for Nothing,* 26

Kryger, Paul, 5, 163n

"Kulaks, The" (later "The Nowaks") (C. I.), 46

"Landauers, The" (C. I.), 12

Lanigan, Mrs., 64, 169n

*Last of Mr. Norris, The,* 3, 45

Laughton, Charles, 143

Lawrence, D. H., 46; "St. Mawr," 138

Lawrence, T. E., 59; *The Odyssey* (translation), 23; *Revolt in the Desert,* 19, 23; *The Seven Pillars of Wisdom,* 19, 23

Lehmann, Beatrix, 147, 155, 159, 177n

Lehmann, John, xii, 25, 29, 46, 48, 67, 79, 160, 166n

Lichtenberg, Bill. *See* de Lichtenberg, Bill

*Life* (magazine), 133

*Life and Letters of Galsworthy, The* (H. V. Marrott), 51

*Lions and Shadows* (C. I.), 43, 87, 97, 108

*Listener, The,* 18, 20, 24, 26, 29, 30, 34, 36, 56, 61, 62, 76, 81

*London Girl in the 80s, The,* 76

*London Mercury,* 24

*Lost, The* (later *Goodbye to Berlin*) (C. I.), 65, 66, 105

Loweth, Mrs., 70, 170n


MacKenzie, Compton, 11, 165n

MacNeice, Louis, 132, 134, 175n

*Madame Curie* (film), 137

Mangeot, André, 81, 84, 164n

Mangeot, Olive, 6, 22, 47, 81, 83, 89, 94, 164n

Mann, Erika, 124, 125, 133, 174n

Mann, Klaus, 3, 18, 34, 125, 143, 165n

Mann, Thomas, 123, 125, 174n

Mann family, 127

Marple Hall, xvi, 89, 104, 133, 164n

Martin Lawrence (publisher), 7

*Mayerling* (film), 79

Mayne, Ethel Colburn, 178n

McFee, James: *Sailor's Wisdom,* 23, 24

Melville, Herman, 47

*Memorial, The* (C. I.), 9, 11, 30, 31

Methuen (publisher), 3, 23, 30, 36, 52, 66

Metro Goldwyn Mayer (MGM), xv, 121, 155; meeting with Samuel Goldwyn, 157, 158, 159

Mitchell, Mrs., 64, 68, 169n

Mitchell, Thea (Miss), 47, 54, 57, 68, 70, 71, 73, 79, 149, 168n

Monkhouse, Allan, 48

Monkhouse, Rachel, 145

Monkhouse family, 20, 37, 166n

Moody, Robert, 67, 72, 79, 81, 170n

*Mr Norris Changes Trains* (C. I.), viii, xi, 3, 6, 9, 11, 14, 13, 25, 27, 31, 32, 45, 52, 64, 68, 131, 159

Munich crisis, 97

Mussolini, Benito, xv, 43, 78

*Mutiny on the Bounty* (film), 79


*Naval Odyssey* (Thomas Woodrooffe), 56, 62

Neddermeyer, Heinz, xiii, xiv, 3, 26, 29, 163n; after arrest, 105, 110, 117, 131, 135, 151; arrest in Trier, 87; birthday, 51; conscription worries, 8, 22, 57; notes to Kathleen, 10, 12, 13, 16, 17, 22, 24, 32, 34, 40; with Mrs. Loweth, 70; operation on nose, 75, 81, 82, 83, 89; in Paris, 87; passport trouble, 5, 13, 16–17, 25, 46, 59; poor eyesight, 30; in Portugal, 39, 62, 67; possible move to South Africa, 10; receives money from Kathleen, 33; trial and sentence, 87

*New Country,* 66

*New Republic,* 133

*News Chronicle,* 111, 112

*New Statesman,* 30, 133

*New Writing,* 46, 48, 61, 67, 79, 156

*New York Times,* 147

Nicolson, Harold, 8, 164n

*North to the Orient* (Anne Morrow Lindbergh), 37

*North West Passage, The* (later *Lions and Shadows*) (C. I.), 81

Norton, Mrs., 48, 171n

"Nowaks, The" (C. I.), 3, 65–66

*Observer,* 23, 26, 50

O'Casey, Sean: *Five Irish Plays,* 51

*Odd Man Out* (Douglas Goldring), 26

*Odyssey, The* (T. E. Lawrence translation), 23

Old, Vernon, 121

*Once Your Enemy,* 74

*On the Frontier* (C. I. with Auden), xiv, 87, 104, 126, 131

Parker, Peter, x–xi, xii, xiii

*Parson's Daughter, A,* 18, 20

*Paul is Alone* (C. I., abandoned), 3, 43, 52, 57, 65

Peacock, Walter, 131

Pearn, Inez, 165n

Penmaenmawr, 152, 154, 160, 175n

Peter Davies (publisher), 23, 30

Phillips, Adam, xi

Prabhavananda, Swami, 121, 177n

*Proletarian Pilgrimage* (John Paton), 46, 51

"Railway Accident, The" (Auden), 83, 172n

Random House (publisher), 121, 123, 127

*Redbook Magazine,* 127

*Rembrandt* (film), 80

*Revolt in the Desert* (T. E. Lawrence), 19, 23

Robson-Scott, William, 25, 32, 64, 70, 83, 94, 166n

Romilly, Giles, 85, 171

Ross, Jean, 79, 81, 84, 171n

Ross, Marjorie, 68, 84, 170n

Russell, Bertrand, 157

*Sabotage* (film), 94

Sackville-West, Vita, 164n

*Sailor's Wisdom* (McFee), 23, 24

Salinger (lawyer), 72, 73, 74, 76, 87, 92, 93, 94, 118, 138, 170n; arrested, 125; sentenced, 143

"Sally Bowles" (C. I.), 43, 79, 87, 106, 108

Scott, Cyril, 140, 176n

Scott-Kilvert, Ian, 67, 105, 106, 107, 155, 170n

*Seven League Boots* (Richard Halliburton), 62–63

*Seven Pillars of Wisdom, The* (T. E. Lawrence), 19, 23, 31

*Shark! Shark!* 46

*Sing Sing Doctor* (Amos O. Squire), 30

*Single Man, A* (C. I.), xvi

*Sir James Sexton, Agitator,* 63

Sloss, Mr., 107

Smith, G. B., 74, 81, 171n

Smollett, Tobias George, 11

Spender, Humphrey, 23, 25, 83, 166n

Spender, Michael, 15, 163n

Spender, Stephen, xi, xiv, 3, 10, 24, 31, 34, 43, 53, 60, 76, 80, 118, 155, 165n; C. I. doesn't hear from him, 129; friend of Lincoln Kirstein, 127; marriage, 82, 83, 85; note to Kathleen, 40; in nursing home, 95; in Spain, 93

*Stagecoach* (film), 144

Stalin, Josef, 140

"St. Mawr" (D. H. Lawrence), 138

*Stars Look Down, The* (A. J. Cronin), 68

Stern, James, xiv, 70–71, 73, 74, 76, 170n

Stern, Tania, xiv, 93, 170n

Surrealism, 77

Symonds (family solicitor), 121

*These Three* (film), 79

*They Walk Alone* (play), 159

*Things Ancient and Modern* (Cyril Alington), 63

*Threepenny Opera,* xiv; C. I. translations, 89–90

Thurau, Meta (Fraulein), 35, 169n

Tolstoy, Leo, 46

Tristram, Leonard, 178n

"Turn Round the World, The" (C. I.), 34

*Unambitious Journey, The* (Theodora Benson), 56

*Under Western Eyes* (film), 79

Upward, Edward, 6, 48, 76, 80, 163n

Van Druten, John, 147, 177n

Viertel, Berthold, 12, 22, 147, 136, 137, 150, 151, 152, 153, 154, 156, 159, 165n, 176n

Viertel, Salka, 137

*Waiting for Nothing* (Kromer), 26

Walpole, Hugh, 7, 14, 164n

Waugh, Evelyn, xi, 113, 174n

*Way of the Transgressor, The* (Negley Farson), 46

Weissmuller, Johnny, 148, 177n

Wentworth, 83

*Where is Francis?* (later *The Dog beneath the Skin*) (C. I. with Auden), 9–10, 11

William Morrow (publisher), 3, 15

Williamson, Henry: *Devon Holiday,* 28

"Winter Term, The" (C. I.), 67

Wintle, Hector, 7, 9, 11, 14, 27, 81, 164n, 165n

Wood, Chris, 125, 130, 136, 131, 175n

Woolf, Leonard, 58–59, 164n

Woolf, Virginia, 164n

Worsley, Cuthbert, 118, 174n

Wyberslegh Hall, 21, 166n

Yeats, W. B., 125

Yoga, 121, 137–38, 140–41, 148–49

Young, Harvey, 121, 134, 139, 143, 145, 152, 154, 156, 175n

**Christopher Isherwood** (1904–1986) is a major figure in both twentieth-century fiction and the gay rights movement. He is best known for his classic *Berlin Stories,* the basis for the stage and movie successes *I Am a Camera* and *Cabaret.* Several of his books are now available in paperback editions from the University of Minnesota Press.

**Lisa Colletta** is assistant professor of English at Babson College in Wellesley, Massachusetts. She is author of *Dark Humor and Social Satire in the Modern British Novel,* as well as various essays on twentieth-century literature.